REMARKABLE

REMARKABLE

STORIES BY

DINAH COX

AMERICAN READER SERIES, NO. 26

BOA EDITIONS, LTD. ❀ ROCHESTER, NY ❀ 2016

First Edition

For information about permission to reuse any material from this book please contact The Permissions Company at www.permissionscompany.com or e-mail permdude@eclipse.net.

Publications by BOA Editions, Ltd.—a not-for-profit corporation under section 501 (c) (3) of the United States Internal Revenue Code—are made possible with funds from a variety of sources, including public funds from the Literature Program of the National Endowment for the Arts; the New York State Council on the Arts, a state agency; and the County of Monroe, NY. Private funding sources include the Lannan Foundation for support of the Lannan Translations Selection Series; the Max and Marian Farash Charitable Foundation; the Mary S. Mulligan Charitable Trust; the Rochester Area Community Foundation; the Steeple-Jack Fund; the Ames-Amzalak Memorial Trust in memory of Henry Ames, Semon Amzalak, and Dan Amzalak; and contributions from many individuals nationwide. See Colophon on page 160 for special individual acknowledgments.

ART WORKS.
arts.gov

State of the Arts

NYSCA

Cover Design: Sandy Knight
Cover Art: *Scape 3* by Anne Havens
Interior Design and Composition: Richard Foerster

BOA Logo: Mirko

Library of Congress Cataloging-in-Publication Data

Names: Cox, Dinah, 1974– author.
Title: Remarkable / Dinah Cox.
Description: Rochester, NY : BOA Editions Ltd., 2016.
Identifiers: LCCN 2015045496 (print) | LCCN 2016001486 (ebook) | ISBN 9781942683100 (paperback) | ISBN 9781942683117 (ebook)
Subjects: LCSH: Eccentrics and eccentricities—Fiction. | High Plains (U.S.)—Fiction. | Oklahoma—Fiction. | Psychological fiction. | BISAC: FICTION / Short Stories (single author). | FICTION / Literary.
Classification: LCC PS3603.O8898 A6 2016 (print) | LCC PS3603.O8898 (ebook) |
DDC 813/.6—dc23
LC record available at http://lccn.loc.gov/2015045496

BOA Editions, Ltd.
250 North Goodman Street, Suite 306
Rochester, NY 14607
www.boaeditions.org
A. Poulin, Jr., Founder (1938–1996)

for Lisa

Contents

Three Small Town Stories

1

A guy walks into Kentucky Fried Chicken and says, *Gimme some chicken.* Maybe he has a gun and maybe he has only his finger, shaking and sweating underneath the front flap of his jacket; either way, his demand is not for money but chicken. Two piece leg and thigh. Extra crispy. No one in his right mind asks for original recipe these days. And that biscuit had better be hot, don't give him any of that hockey puck shit. Everyone is worried. Once, exactly a year ago today, a tornado ripped through town and blew out the restaurant's front windows. Customers, clerks, managers, babies, and dead frozen chickens all huddled in the walk-in for safety. No one was hurt. But today is a different story. If the man with the gun/finger doesn't get his chicken, he might shoot someone. He might kill someone.

"To go," he says. "Didn't I say *to go* earlier? I think I did."

"You did, sir," says the clerk. "Sorry."

"Damn right you're sorry."

This is where the story begins and also where the

story ends, because the guy took his chicken and left the store. Just walked right out. And no one called the police and no one posted about it on Facebook and no one tweeted or bleated or cared. The register didn't even come up short because no money changed hands. But the best part of the story is that it at once represents what's best about small towns and what's worst about them. What's best is that people in small towns will give one another chicken. For free. What's worst is the tornado's near miss, the broken glass all over the greasy floor, the children crying, the dead chickens in the freezer, and the people who want nothing more than to eat them.

2

Melissa and Shane are sweethearts. Melissa and Shane are in love. They met when they were twelve and thirteen, but now they're both in college, home for the summer between their freshman and sophomore years. Melissa is majoring in elementary education; Shane hasn't yet decided what he's majoring in, but he's thinking about Livestock Merchandising, Sports Management, or Art. Today they're passengers on a hayride, only without the hay.

"This is much better anyway," Melissa says. "Hay is really itchy."

"They could have thrown in some rejects," Shane says. "Damn."

Indeed the hayride is a miserable affair, amounting to little more than an open stock trailer, its rusted metal frame and black rubber flooring both searing hot against the noonday sun, pulled by a lazy antique tractor better off dead in some old codger's barn. The old codger himself is driving the tractor; Shane and Melissa take their seats in the back. Shane takes off his shirt and offers it to Melissa to sit on. She accepts, and they watch the town go by slowly, at about five miles per hour. Liquor store, Baptist church, Church of the Savior, miniature golf course (closed due to arson), storefront church called "God's Garage," Mexican restaurant (closed until further notice), bingo hall, high school, hair salon (really someone's living room), Subway sandwich shop, football field, church. Melissa likes it here and wants to return after college. Shane does not like it here, but Melissa hopes he is coming around. Aside from the driver, they are alone on this hayride, everyone else in town too hot or too smart to leave their houses after coming home from church. They roll past the convenience store where they had their first date, past the dog pound where they volunteered to raise money for the senior class, past the water tower, now winking a lonely red light to signal impotence or dread, all summer long the pressure has been low, the lawns brittle and brown, the faucets reduced to a trickle, the dogs kept indoors, the hay prices gone through the roof. For the first time, Melissa puts together the fact of the terrible weather and the hayless hayride—maybe this was all they could find or afford. She feels both sad and driven to action; she and Shane, together so young and strong and with so much time on their hands, surely there's something they can do. In her mind's eye, she's planning a spaghetti dinner, something simple and rustic, a fundraiser for all those stricken by the drought. She's imagining Shane, cutting up behind the counter, donning a chef's hat and waving a wooden spoon, Italian music in the background, a shiny napkin dispenser at his elbow, cloth tablecloths laundered for the occasion, the authenticity of the Old World, the charity of the new. She's just about to speak her fantasy aloud when the tractor's gears grind in a wretched squeal, a lurch forward, then back, then forward again, the long, high whine of mechanical failure still an echo in her ears. She grabs Shane's arm and asks him what's going on.

"Brakes," Shane says. "This shit is *old*."

They're stopped now, and Melissa wants to go home. She sees the shadow of the tree line in both directions, rabbit brush and sage, black-eyed Susans gone to seed, the dry creek bed dotted with plantain weeds and bark from the river birch leaning over them from the bank. She realizes at once they're outside the city limits, still close enough to walk, but without water they'd have to stop at the convenience store on the way. She wonders if Shane remembered to bring his phone or his wallet, since she, planning a lazy day in his company, left hers on the dresser at home. The old man driving the tractor is familiar—everyone is at least sort of familiar around here—but she doesn't know his name. She thinks he's her friend Kelsey's great-uncle from back east, but she's not sure. Shane will know what to do.

"You need a hand?" Shane hollers to the driver.

"Sit tight," the driver says. "She needs to rest here for a bit. In the shade."

They're quiet for a while, and a single cloud, like

a tablecloth freshly laundered for the occasion, passes over the sun. Melissa looks up to see a deer, a young one, thin and beautiful and silent, drinking what should be water but is really cottonwood hulls from the creek bed below. Shane, too, sees the deer. He does not move or speak. It's anybody's guess whether or not the driver— who really is Kelsey's great-uncle from back east—sees the deer, because his future is already sealed: television and frozen dinners and too many naps in the middle of the afternoon. But in that exact moment, Shane decides he will major in Livestock Merchandising, and Melissa, changed by the deer's sudden grace, decides she will change her major to Art.

3

The man who killed himself is the same man who used the garden hose every morning to fill the concrete bird-bath in the backyard. The man who killed himself is the same man who baked peanut butter pies but never ate them, insisting he was watching his weight. The man who killed himself is the same man who never went to a restaurant without his own fork, knife, and spoon. The man who killed himself is the same man who killed his son's goldfish and then lied and said it was already dead. The man who killed himself is the same man who liked to go bowling, in a traveling league, the same man who wouldn't let anyone but his wife see his closet full of bowling shirts and four very expensive bowling balls. Not that anyone ever asked to see inside his closet because they didn't. The man who killed himself was handsome, except for his nose and his teeth. The man who killed himself was a magician, but only in his dreams. The man who killed himself is on fire, and that's how he killed himself, like Richard Pryor did, only faster and with more success. The man who killed himself is not to be pitied because he did some terrible things. The man who killed himself ought to be glad he's getting out of this hellhole where nothing ever happens, nothing ever happens, nothing ever happens not even after he's dead.

Adolescence in B Flat

The Telephone Museum is always empty. Marcella, who is embarrassed to tell people her job is to answer the telephone at the Telephone Museum, does schoolwork during her shifts. No one ever calls. Sometimes, late at night, after the doors are locked and the security guard has gone home for the evening, Marcella abandons the carpeted reception area, walks out onto the hardwood floors of the museum proper, past the curator's office, and, finally, downstairs into the tangled mess of the switchboard room.

The basement, once a state-of-the-art interactive display center, now left to the dust mites, reminds Marcella of the music library in her orchestra classroom at school. The gallery's low ceiling makes her feel smaller, more easily hidden under the single shadow cast by a desk lamp near the doorway. Ground level windows glow with light from the streetlights outside. Marcella sits in a wooden library seat, her history textbook propped under the chair's broken leg. She tucks her hair behind her ears and dons headphones, large, padded pillows that drown out the late night sounds of the city traffic. Sometimes she waits a long time before she hears a double click, followed by static, and somewhere very far away, voices, one a man's, the other, a woman's.

The man's voice says, "Keep quiet at dinner next time, will you? Not every thought in your head merits discussion."

"The Shockleys didn't seem to mind."

"They were just being nice."

"Most people are interested in gardening."

"Most people are interested in themselves. No one needs a lecture on soil drainage."

Then, abruptly, the conversation stops. Marcella marvels at the couple's honesty. Married people must possess the freedom to speak without hesitation or fear. She waits another couple of minutes or so, and then, another conversation, this time between two men.

"You wanna play ball?"

"Basketball?"

"No, bowling ball, stupid. Wadda ya think?"

"I don't wanna."

"Why?"

"You called me stupid."

"You are stupid."

"So are you."

"You wanna play ball?"

Marcella listens for a while longer and hears nothing but static. She presses the headphones to her ears and leans into the console, closer, she thinks, to the site of transmission. At home, her mother will be waiting up. Any minute now, she will step onto the front porch and call Marcella's name. She will return to the living room, position herself on the exact middle of the sofa, and look straight ahead at the television's empty screen. Marcella and her mother own several dozen home appliances, all broken: television, hi-fi stereo, electric drill. Someday, Marcella thinks, she will pack all the dead soldiers— blender, hand-held vacuum, pencil sharpener—into a trash bag and heave the entire bundle into the back of her uncle's pickup truck: a statement, she thinks, an act of defiance.

Marcella returns to the Telephone Museum's reception area and stacks her belongings into a picnic basket, a crumbling relic she found in the dumpster behind the gas station next door. Only a backpack designed for camping and youthful journeys across Europe would be big enough for all Marcella carries: half a dozen library books, four three-ring binders for school, and a sculpture-in-progress made from tongue depressors and glue. Working on the sculpture takes up hours of Marcella's weekend. She must finish the project not for the benefit of an art class but for a required early morning session called Twenty-first Century Focus and Achievement. Lugging the picnic basket all the way home makes her shoulders ache, but Marcella cannot think of a better system. Her mother has suggested a bicycle, but Marcella would rather walk. She has seen bicycle riders expressing deliberate exhaustion as they hunch over handlebars and toss back handfuls of trail mix, a look Marcella doesn't think she would be able to pull off. Instead, she does what her mother calls "hoofing it," coming home late to her mother's pronouncement that her "dogs must be barking."

On the way home, she stops to look at the computers

in the display window at Circuit City. Someday, she wants a laptop to carry in her picnic basket. For now, she does all her assignments on her uncle's Macintosh, and prints the results on his old dot matrix printer, a white box the size of a toaster oven. Neither her uncle nor Marcella's mother believes in what Marcella's Focus and Achievement teacher calls the Awesome Power of the Internet. Marcella tries to explain to her uncle and mother about progress. These days, she tells her mother, teachers expect their students to log onto the school's website to check for new assignments. If a field trip requires a permission slip, parents must download the signature slip and print the liability information from their home computers. Marcella, embarrassed to bring in her mother's handwritten approval—*Marcella has my permission to go to Orchestra Contest in Enid. 372-5120. Annette Shreve*—takes the ill-conceived missive to the dumpster behind the gas station next door to the Telephone Museum and lets her mother's backward scrawl float to the bottom of a rusted-out drum. She stops in the school library before homeroom, downloads the official paperwork, forges her mother's signature, and dons the disguise of a normal student of the new millennium.

"I've been wondering about you," says Marcella's mother one night, late, after Marcella's shift at the Telephone Museum. "Did you hear me calling?"

Marcella's mother, defiantly a chain-smoker in the age of lung cancer, stands on the edge of the front porch. Most people—men, usually—say Marcella and her mother look like sisters. Their spare bedroom houses her mother's younger brother, a one-time lead singer for heavy metal bar bands who ekes out a living working on the loading dock at a local business establishment called Remarkable Lamps. Marcella wonders if the neighbors think the three of them orphans, escapees from the city center for misguided youth.

"Mom," says Marcella. She drops her picnic basket on a lawn chair by the garage. "The museum stops selling admission tickets at nine. I have to stay and close up."

"Tell me another one," her mother says. "You have school tomorrow."

Ignoring this familiar admonition, Marcella brushes past her mother into the crowded entryway. Their house, literally overflowing with cardboard boxes full of her uncle's guitar magazines, traps Marcella in a maze of coffee tables and wicker furniture. Marcella must step sideways to navigate the outer edges of the living room. Her bedroom, which is really not a bedroom at all, but a curtained-off corner of the laundry room, stays awake when the rest of the house sleeps. At night, long after her mother and uncle have gone to bed, Marcella stays up to work on her tongue depressor sculpture, a project, her teacher tells her, designed to stress the importance of following directions.

"Don't walk away from me, Marcella," her mother says, following Marcella past the broken television set, into the kitchen, and finally between the parted curtains leading to Marcella's fortress of fabric softener and books. "This telephone museum thing needs to stop."

Marcella doesn't want to tell her mother about the voices she hears in the switchboard gallery at the museum. Already a family friend has diagnosed Marcella with Attention Deficit Disorder and a lazy eye. Additional craziness on Marcella's part would only confirm the oft-talked-about worry that Marcella, such a pretty little thing, lacks romantic companionship. Her uncle, whenever he relaxes into one of his rare good moods, calls her Marcella, the Rose in the Desert.

"I like the Telephone Museum," Marcella says, allowing a new box of tongue depressors to spill open with a clatter on top of the washing machine. "I learn stuff there."

"I learn stuff at my job, too," her mother says. Marcella's mother, sitting behind bulletproof glass, works as a dispatcher for the local police station. She, too, listens to the personal details of telephone calls from strangers. Once, when Marcella came home to find a package of ground beef defrosting on the countertop, she called the police station to ask her mother if she should start dinner. Speeding through the conversation in a low tone Marcella didn't recognize, her mother told Marcella not to cry wolf on the taxpayer's dime. Hamburger meat, she said, hardly counts as an emergency.

Her mother situates herself on the laundry room's windowsill and continues, "Nothing wrong with getting a little education in the workplace. But I'm talking about human interaction, Marcella. I'm talking about real life."

"There's real life at the Telephone Museum." By now Marcella has taken the carpenter's glue from a shelf above the dryer. The sculpture assignment, though burdensome, has a necessary calming effect on Marcella before she goes to sleep.

"I'm not talking about pay phones behind velvet ropes," her mother says. "You need to spend time with people your own age."

"All right," Marcella promises. "I'll join the pep club at school."

"Don't be smart."

"You were in the pep club, weren't you?" Marcella says. "When you were in high school?"

"We didn't call it the pep club," her mother says. "Goodnight. Don't stay up all night working on that thing."

When her mother pulls the curtain closed in the doorway of the laundry room, Marcella listens for signs of life in the kitchen. She hears the hinges squeak on her mother's bedroom door. Her uncle, who seems to take a vow of silence every day after the sun goes down, pounds a fist on the broken microwave oven. Grateful the washing machine still works, Marcella puts in a load of blue jeans and sets the dial for industrial clean. Doing so, she knows, will annoy her uncle and cause him to pound additional broken home appliances, but she needs something to wear for school tomorrow and, like the maiden trapped in the tower, Marcella imagines every crack in the castle's foundation will one day hasten her escape. She looks through a hole in the curtain hovering between her room and the kitchen and watches as her uncle drops the frying pan into the sink. By the time the washing machine starts the rinse cycle, he has ripped the broken box fan from its secure spot in the kitchen window and overturned a planter full of seashells from the beach. Finally, he grabs a metal tin from a cabinet above the sink, dumps saltine crackers onto a plate, and settles down at the kitchen table to look at the day's mail. Marcella knows he wants to win a mail-in sweepstakes and buy his own house. He enters all the contests: Publishers Clearing House, American Family Winners, Who Wants to Be a Millionaire. Unlucky in love, he imagines himself a bargain-maker when wheeling and dealing in the risky world of money. The washing machine buzzes, and the house, except for the dryer's low hum, sleeps through the night. Marcella, her fingers sticky with carpenter's glue, stays awake for hours.

"Good morning, students," Mr. Bramlett says. He wears a necktie under his overalls, a mix-and-match combo, he says, to add professionalism to the practicality of the common man. "I trust everyone completed the online Career Path to Tomorrow Hands-on Quiz? Yes? Marcella?"

"No," she says.

"No?"

Marcella, who sits in the back of the classroom with her face hidden behind her picnic basket, resents Mr. Bramlett's persistent interest in her home life. Mr. Bramlett, a thirty-something bachelor who plays in a garage band with Marcella's uncle, spends a good deal of time staring at Marcella's legs. Back in the day when her mother's television was operational, Marcella saw a news program about driver's education teachers—football and basketball coaches, probably—who took their students on wild excursions, flying through stop signs and renting hotel rooms in neighboring towns. If Mr. Bramlett ever tried to invite Marcella to a video arcade or an ice cream parlor, she would notify the authorities. For now, she provides only brief answers to his too-jolly questions.

"No," she says again. "Sorry."

"You're telling me, Marcella, you have yet to complete your Career Path to Tomorrow Hands-on Quiz?"

"Yes."

"What's going to happen to you, Marcella, when your Career Path leads to the City of Failure?"

The other students, though no particular friends of Marcella, still appear uncomfortable on her behalf. Motionless in their chairs, they turn their collective gaze to the classroom floor.

"I don't know," she says.

"You don't know?"

"Right."

"Well," Mr. Bramlett says. "I'll see you after school then."

Marcella tries to tell Mr. Bramlett about her field trip to the orchestra contest in Enid: students have received instructions to board the bus during fifth hour, perform sight-reading exercises in Enid High School's closet-sized practice rooms, and return home again some time after dark. But Mr. Bramlett has already moved on to another lesson. Marcella does not pay attention. Instead, she closes her eyes and returns to the dark cavern of the Telephone Museum, the only place, she thinks, where she has any time alone. Sometimes, when she finishes with envelope-licking duties in the reception area, she carries a clipboard around to all the galleries and takes inventory. Every glass case and wooden shelf, dusty from years of neglect, comes under her scrutiny. The floors, buckled with uneven slopes in the doorways, glisten with a noticeable lack of footprints. Silk banners hang from the ceilings of the more contemporary galleries—the ones with the framed color photographs of businessmen breaking ground on the corporate children and grandchildren of AT&T—but the older parts of the museum, the hideaway holes where Marcella spends most of her time, receive little attention from the interior decorator. She hears echoes with every footfall.

Tucked behind a mop in the switchboard room's custodial closet is a worn, hand-painted sign, *Interactive Learning: More Than Ten Thousand Real-Life Conversations Recorded Live Throughout the Twentieth Century*. The trained professionals in charge of the Telephone Museum—the exhibit designers, department heads, even the curator—all live under the impression the switchboard room is now defunct. Marcella knows better. Headphones secure around her ears, she sits in her favorite wooden chair, pushes a red button on the switchboard console, and hears a woman's throaty backcountry voice saying, "Sheriff?"

No answer, then static, then a double-click.

"Sheriff, I need your help."

"What's the trouble, ma'am?"

The woman's voice turns tinny, robotic. She speaks as if performing in a talent show for cult members.

"Sheriff, I need your help."

"We're here for you, ma'am. Is someone in your house?"

"Sheriff, I need your help."

Marcella, unsure if the woman on the recording truly suffers from the effects of panic or if the switchboard interactive display is even more defective than anyone knows, pushes another button on the console. Flipping a switch, she hears static, then silence. She presses the headphones closer to her ears. More static and then a long buzz. Three short clicks, and then she hears a man's voice, clear as day.

"Marcella," he says. He sounds young, but of another era, like one of those hairless heartthrobs in surfing movies from the 1960s. "Marcella," he says again, and this time there's a lilt to his voice, as if he might burst into song. She leans into the console and turns the volume control knob as far to the right as it will go. Very softly, far away, she hears the sounds of a crowd bursting into applause. In spite of the man's voice saying her name a third time, she wonders for a moment about the extent of her own powers of imagination. If she's conjuring these voices from thin air, if they're merely flights of fancy, she doesn't mind, really—why not? Sometimes, others take very seriously matters Marcella considers trivial, or worse, they work themselves into a lather staging morality plays for an audience of one. If the voices in the Telephone Museum are little more than leftover electrical charges from her waking dreams, well then, so much the better. At least she *has* waking dreams.

"Marcella," the man's voice says again. "B Flat."

"What?" she says aloud. There's no microphone to

speak into, but she pushes a red button that says Intercom. No one will hear her, but it seems the right thing to do.

"B Flat," the man's voice says again. "Don't forget now, B Flat."

She considers the possibility the man's voice is saying "Be Flat," as in "Be good" or "Be careful" rather than—her initial impression—offering some mysterious clue into her future as a violinist.

She releases the intercom button and speaks into the air conditioning vent on the floor near her feet. "Be flat yourself," she says. "Go on now, be flat."

"Beee Flat," the man's voice says again, faintly, just above the sound of the crowd's applause, now building to a crescendo of whistles and cheers. "Marcella," he continues, crooning. "The world is round. Apples are round. Baseballs: round. You, Marcella. Be Flat."

Anger wells up inside her as she rises from her chair and takes off the headphones. "Sheriff," she says aloud. "I need your help."

Her voice goes unanswered. She hears only her own unsteady footsteps and the mechanical hum of the breathing building as the halls rumble with the air conditioner's aging motor. She walks through the long gallery, turning off the lights above the display cases as she goes. Back in the reception area, she discovers an uneaten sandwich on top of one of the file cabinets—the security guard must have forgotten his dinner. She opens the file cabinet and files the sandwich under S—a joke, though not a very funny one, for herself alone, since she's never seen anyone else open the file cabinet. She turns off the lights in the reception area and pats her pocket for her keys. The room is suddenly so pitch black she cannot see her own hand in front of her face. Just to make sure, she hooks together her thumbs and flutters her fingers, an invisible butterfly aloft in the dark.

At the orchestra contest in Enid, Marcella is surprised to see both Mr. Bramlett and her uncle listed as judges on the printed program issued to all contest participants. Both men consider themselves local experts on the stand-up bass. Marcella, her violin tucked under her arm, stares down at the program. She has always hated Mr. Bramlett's first name: Elic. Not Eric, but Elic, as in Smart Alec, only with an E. Why had Mr. Bramlett asked Marcella to stay in his classroom after school? Maybe he knew all along Marcella would be unable to complete the Career Path to Tomorrow Hands-on Quiz and, wise with the knowledge their paths would cross again at the orchestra contest, he thought he might cut to the chase and offer her a ride to Enid in his truck. Why is *he* the judge, anyway? Marcella knows the administrators at Enid High School are notoriously cheap; probably they failed to find any respectable judges and, in a moment of desperation, offered Mr. Bramlett and Marcella's uncle each a meager paycheck consisting of a handshake and a twenty-dollar gift certificate to Music Madness in the mall. For this, the deadbeat orchestra alumni would award first and second place respectively to Andrea Seabrook and Tan Ly, the only two bass players who managed to show up for today's contest.

Marcella, playing scales in the corner of the gymnasium, wonders at her own misfortune. Nervous, she adds resin to her bow. Her orchestra teacher, a man much older and considerably more sedate than Mr. Bramlett, has told her years of practice and a dozen or so superior ratings at contests like this one might someday help her get into a conservatory. She practices at school, practices at home, practices in a remote corner of the Telephone Museum. But when Marcella gets to a contest, she freezes and plays like a rank beginner. A rating of "excellent" is the best she can hope for.

"Marcella," Mr. Bramlett says. He stands behind a table and passes out free Enid High School hand towels. "I should have known. Your career, I see, belongs to the age of Mozart."

Marcella refuses a hand towel and instead takes a couple of free pencils from an open box on the table. "Can I have a name tag?" she says. "We're supposed to have name tags."

Mr. Bramlett—his name tag says Elic—passes Marcella a blank white sticker and a Sharpie marker. "Be sure to write Marcella, the Rose in the Desert."

Marcella writes "Marcie" in large block letters and "violin" in smaller letters below. "Thank you," she says, placing the name tag on the uppermost part of her shoulder. She wouldn't dream of sticking anything to her chest. She pretends to head for the gymnasium's double doors, but instead ducks into a secret position at the back of the concession stand line. Still close enough to the hand towel table to hear Mr. Bramlett's boisterous laugh, she watches as her uncle descends from the uppermost row in a long wall of bleachers. Framed by a pair of basketball goals, he carries with him a clipboard and a CD jewel case.

"This is it," he says, waving the jewel case in the air. "You have to hear this."

At first, Marcella thinks her uncle is talking to her. Could he have spied her in the concession stand line? She watches as he runs down the steps without looking to check his footfalls beneath. Quickly, she realizes he's heading for Mr. Bramlett. Neither man seems aware of her presence nearby.

"I've heard it all," says Mr. Bramlett. "Some kid thinks he's the next Jaco Pastorius. You want a hand towel?"

"This is for real."

Mr. Bramlett says, "You think so? Get this man a free sample bag."

Marcella's uncle says, "Live from the Blue Coyote. Last weekend?"

"Yeah?"

"You and me, buddy. And the other guys. Bet you didn't know the place was wired."

"Tell me another one."

"No shit, man. They got the crowd noise and everything."

The Blue Coyote, Marcella knows, enjoys a fine reputation, its large dance floor and shimmering wallpaper attracting hordes of the young urban elite. That her uncle and Mr. Bramlett could score a gig there in the first place is big news indeed. If this recording possesses any real potential, Marcella doubts the speed of the band's rise to Top Forty fame. Her uncle seems always in search of the next big deal. Marcella knows better than to believe him.

"Well, let's hear it, then," Mr. Bramlett says. Marcella steps out of the concession stand line and starts for the long hallways leading to the practice rooms. Behind her, she overhears the last of their conversation. They make plans to go over song titles at dinner later in the week.

"My house," says Marcella's uncle. "My sister will be at work."

"And the kid?"

"Telephone Museum, probably. If she shows up later on we'll stick her in the laundry room."

So much they know. The Telephone Museum is closed on Fridays.

"Nah," Mr. Bramlett says. "She's all right."

All right, indeed. Once, when Marcella was thirteen, her uncle threw a party while her mother was in Miami for a law enforcement convention. Marcella tried to stay out of the way, but one of her uncle's friends, a man wearing a T-shirt that said *No Shirt, No Shoes, No Problem*, talked her into having a couple of beers. She doesn't remember what happened next, only her mother's unexpected cheerfulness upon her return. Neither the broken dishes nor the stains on the carpet made her the least bit angry. She didn't say "boys will be boys," but in Marcella's mind, her mother might as well have bought her uncle a subscription to *Playboy* magazine.

With Mr. Bramlett on her mind, Marcella earns only a rating of "good" during the sight-reading competition. She receives not a certificate with a foil sticker in the corner but a bookmark-sized comment sheet telling her to learn to relax. On the bus ride home, she thinks about taking the Career Path to Tomorrow Hands-on Quiz. The computer will ask her questions such as: Would you rather fix a flat tire or take a friend on a rock collecting expedition? Marcella would like to answer by saying, "I would rather kill myself than fix a flat tire *or* take a friend on a rock collecting expedition," but this choice is not allowed. Everyone would like Marcella to become a pillar of the community or, failing that, the wife of a pillar of the community. Her mother, so full of the daisy grower's perpetual need for sunlight, makes Marcella feel as if she might never learn to chat with other people with any real degree of personal charm. Mr. Bramlett's class is supposed to help her learn to believe in the future, to focus on achievement, to network, to find fault only with those sour women who dare to find fault.

But Marcella likes to find fault. The only part of Mr. Bramlett's class she actually enjoys is the unit on following directions. The instruction sheets, usually packed with misinformation or unnecessary steps, remind Marcella of her favorite command on the keyboard of her uncle's Apple computer: open apple A followed by the backspace key; three quick finger strokes and everything disappears.

Rummaging through her picnic basket on the bus ride home, she cannot bear to think of herself standing before the board of directors somewhere talking about growth potential. Married to the chairman of the board, she would have to host dinner parties and attend fundraisers, and, at home, sleep with someone always grouchy from work. More growth potential. She would have to engage in pillow talk always thematically linked to growth potential. Marcella doesn't want to grow. She wants to shrink.

The next day at the Telephone Museum, the security guard calls in sick and the curator leaves early to attend her daughter's school play. Marcella promises to dust the early cell phones and restock the postcard rack, but she knows at once she will shirk both duties and sneak off to the Switchboard Room.

She turns off all the lights. Blindness, she reasons, will improve her ability to hear the faraway voices. She presses a single button, and the console glows green. She flips a switch marked "receive." Better to receive than to give. Better to give than to deceive.

Right away, she realizes it's a busy night on the switchboard. Several conversations are occurring at once—each voice seems unaware of the others, unaware of the years gone by, the miles between them, the pointless question of whether their conversations are real or make-believe. At first, she recognizes some of her old favorites—the boys who want to play ball, the Be Flat singer, the woman who embarrassed her husband at the dinner party.

"Damn right I wanna play ball."

"Tractor tires are round."

"I'm never making dinner again."

"Marcella . . ."

"What kinda idiot plays ball in this heat?"

"The only thing you're good for is making dinner."

"A man's head is round."

"Look who you're calling an idiot."

The woman begins to cry.

The man slams a door.

The boys bounce a ball in the driveway.

"Marcella," the singer croons. "Bee Flat."

She flips the switch away from "receive" and toward "standby." Static pops in her ears—more buzzing—and then: silence. She decides right then she is going to break the switchboard console, with a hammer if she has to. Maybe it will suffice to open the control panel and cut a few wires. In any case, she wants nothing more to do with these voices, these damaged shadows from the past. Maybe her mother is right: she ought to join the pep club at school. In her mind, she hears the quick, skipping notes of a piece she's been rehearsing for orchestra class, one of those easy-to-read scores meant for schoolchildren and beginners: "Russian Sailor's Dance." She dances in the halls of the Telephone Museum. She dances in secret on the long walk home.

"I brought you something," says Mr. Bramlett when Marcella walks in her own front door. Her uncle's stereo speakers are blaring some kind of electric sizzle, a singer—her uncle probably—screaming *Please don't hurt me* in time to a pounding bass drum. A box of her uncle's guitar magazines has been dumped out on the coffee table and Mr. Bramlett, sweaty and straining on a stepladder, is repairing the broken ceiling fan in the center of the living room. "Go look on the washing machine," he says.

When Marcella calls him by name and says thank you, Mr. Bramlett tells her to call him Elic.

"Thank you," she says again. "Elic."

"Nice of you to call me by my first name," he says, reaching for a screwdriver in his back pocket. "But you haven't seen it yet."

In the laundry room, on top of a pile of her uncle's folded T-shirts, Marcella finds a laptop computer still wrapped in plastic from the store. She doesn't know what to do. In the kitchen, her uncle slams the phonebook against the wall. Marcella hears him mutter something like, "no good pizza in this town anymore." The loud music and the now whirring ceiling fan continue in the living room.

"You're welcome," Mr. Elic Bramlett says over her shoulder. "You like?" He touches her shoulder and breathes next to her ear.

On a rampage, her uncle bursts into the laundry room and takes Marcella's tongue depressor sculpture from the shelf above the dryer. He drops it to the floor and crushes it with his foot.

"You asshole," Marcella says. "I made that."

"It's all right, Marcella," says Mr. Bramlett. "I'll give you extra time to make another one."

By now, both Mr. Bramlett's hands are on both Marcella's shoulders. Marcella's uncle seems not to notice. "The music, Elic," he says. "Listen to that smooth sound." Marcella pulls away from Mr. Bramlett and runs into the kitchen. She dials her mother at work.

"Come home," she tells her mother. "I need you."

"Marcella," her mother says. "I told you not to call this number."

"This is serious," she says.

"I'll be home later," her mother says, before Marcella can finish. "Tell your uncle I'll pick up a pizza on my way home. And turn down the music, all right? Look, I have to go."

"Mom," says Marcella. "I need help."

"Goodbye," says her mother. "Chin up."

Three Sad Stories

1

The first story is about a guy named Alan McAvoy. He's short and blond, looks like a Ken doll except with lines around his mouth and gray at the temples. Also, he's much thinner than a Ken doll, and his bones seem to suffer from a lack of calcium. Aside from the wrinkles and gray hair and small, thin frame, he's a Ken doll all the way; even his feet seem to belong in sneakers. He and his wife work for a company that provides entertainment for children's birthday parties. It's humiliating, but they dress up like theme park characters—bunnies, rodents, friendly dinosaurs—and walk around shaking hands and passing out balloons. Before every party, they sign contracts that say they're not allowed to speak.

One day, they worked this rich kid's party—it wasn't even his birthday. "Just to celebrate," his mother said, "you know, boyhood." So the pint-sized guests swung at a piñata, ate gourmet hot dogs, and bounced around on top of a depressed-looking, broken-down old pony. The party was winding down when the rich kid whose non-birthday it was came up to Alan McAvoy's wife and started pulling on her tail. He yanked hard, too, so the tail almost came off in his hand. At first, Alan just shook his finger at the boy as if to say, "naughty, naughty." But then the boy began to gesticulate wildly, swinging his hips as if he were a dancer in a music video, grabbing his crotch and thrusting himself at Alan's bewildered wife. When the boy grabbed her breast, Alan grabbed the boy's collar and squatted to meet his gaze. "I'll kick your ass," he said to the boy. "You hear me?"

The sad part of the story is I am Alan McAvoy's wife. My name is Tracy McAvoy. Later, after we went home and hung our costumes in the closet, he wouldn't speak to me, not even after I made his favorite falafel sandwich for dinner. He spent the remainder of the evening looking online for casting calls, and when I went to the bedroom to phone my sister, I'll admit it, I cried.

2

I'm generally not the kind of person who believes wishes can come true, so when I phoned the Make-A-Wish Foundation and lied about my kid having cancer, it was not without some trepidation. At first, I felt terrible, like this woman I know from work. A few months ago, she had to miss a big meeting, so she lied and said her uncle died when really she wanted to take three days off to attend a Star Trek convention in a faraway state. Right in the middle of Leonard Nimoy's big speech, her cell phone rang, and though she didn't pick up, she found out later her uncle really *had* died, though it was not the same uncle she had been thinking of. Of course, she couldn't help but feel as if she had invited his death, and she never skipped another big meeting at work again, not even for her uncle's funeral. So with that in mind, I felt pretty bad, like my kid would get cancer for sure, but I guess I had a little insurance since he's in his late twenties, in great shape, a marathon-runner, in fact, and he lives in California, very far away from here. Not that living in California automatically keeps people from getting cancer, but still, people there drink a lot of wheat grass juice and that kind of thing, so I wasn't worried.

The next day, I decided to remove the wallpaper in my extra bathroom. I don't know if you've ever tried removing wallpaper, but it is no picnic. At first, I sprayed on a mixture of three parts water and one part Downy liquid fabric softener, but the wallpaper, like an enormous postage stamp from a foreign land, stuck like glue—well, it *was* glue—to the crumbling plaster of my poor bathroom walls. So off I went to the hardware store to buy this bottle of blue gelatinous liquid, an anti-enzymatic mixture meant to help remove wallpaper with ease. I read the small print, because I always read the small print, and I just about fell off the edge of the bathtub when I arrived at the part that said, "may cause cancer in the state of California." So that's when I called back the Make-A-Wish Foundation and said yes, my kid was in remission, no, he didn't need to have dinner with Mick Jagger, and no, he didn't actually need anyone to come to our house to help install a rain barrel and maybe clean out the gutters.

And wouldn't you know it, the sappy woman at the

Make-A-Wish Foundation wouldn't believe me.

"You poor man," she said. "We have some phone numbers you can call."

I didn't want her phone numbers, and I told her so, and things started to get a little testy when she finally admitted they had been having trouble getting Jagger anyway, but they were sending someone over to help with the rain barrel whether I liked it or not.

Turned out the guy they sent over actually *looked* a little like Mick Jagger, though I don't think that was part of the plan.

"I bet you get the Mick Jagger thing all the time," I said. He was on a ladder, I was on the roof.

"It's the lips," he said. "Too much chaw."

I said, "You ever tried one of these rain barrel things?"

"Nope," he said.

"You think the Make-A-Wish Foundation will help pay for a new roof? I mean, my kid has cancer. He lives in California, but still."

"The way I see it," he said. "The Foundation will pay for half your roof. The other half you'll have to pay for yourself."

I just about pushed him off the roof for saying that, I don't know why. But then we finished with the gutters and went inside for a beer. He went home, I put some food in the microwave, watched a little television. Maybe this will sound stupid, but I felt very happy when I hit the "mute" button on the remote, started dozing off on the sofa, and heard the sweet-sweet sound of raindrops hitting the driveway outside.

3

This is a story about e-mail. Already you're feeling sad, maybe a little bored. Ella, too, feels sad and bored and maybe a little guilty every time she checks her e-mail. Ella is 33, too old to enjoy herself, too young and too broke to worry about an IRA. (Although a recent unsolicited e-mail message reminded her she's never too young to start planning for retirement.) This is also a story about retirement, a retirement party, actually, an occasion for melancholy masquerading as fun. A man she knows from work is retiring. And maybe he's too young to retire, and maybe he's not. Maybe he's been having seizures, maybe his haircut isn't what it used to be, maybe his wife is somewhat younger and considerably more accomplished than he, maybe he has a little dog, a Tibetan terrier who prefers his wife to him. You've heard this kind of story before. Every day, an e-mail message arrives in Ella's inbox reminding her to stop by a certain secretary's office in order to contribute to the retirement gift fund. The "party kitty" as it has become known, also asks its contributors to consider the high cost of catering and the necessity for an open bar. The gift itself is a set of rare books in French, and though Ella doesn't speak French, she knows the retiring man fancies himself sophisticated, and will indeed appreciate receiving such finery. In addition, the retiring man is a friend of the family, a distant uncle of sorts, a man who once gave Ella a ride home from junior high school in his fuel-efficient luxury sedan, an air-conditioned cave with plush seats and tinted windows wherein she was made to listen to him recite some of his recently-written haiku. So she feels some affection for the retiring man, but she knows from experience retirement parties nearly always leave people wanting to shoot themselves, and well, she's out of money for the month, too. She knows, also from experience, never to go around the office blabbing about how broke you are, because doing so only makes the people who pay you feel guilty they're not paying you enough, and before you know it, their guilt turns to rage and they, your bosses, start to suspect you're looking for another job or maybe drinking coffee without dropping a quarter in the dish. As a result, Ella avoids the secretary collecting money, avoids the pressure to RSVP, avoids thinking about the retirement party at all.

Until one day the retiring man stops her in front of the newspaper machine outside and says, "Are you coming to my party?"

"Yes," she says, but I won't eat anything, and I'll only drink water."

"That sounds good," he says.

"You want a newspaper?" she says, holding the machine's door open for that extra second in which another paper can be grabbed for free.

"Nah," he says. "I'm trying to get rid of stuff like that."

"Newspapers?"

"Newspapers, books, too much stuff. You ought to come to my office and take what you want."

This reminds Ella of another friend of the family, one who survived small town life by wearing large hats and pink lipstick every day of the week. Finally, sick of her own possessions, she threw a "house cooling" party upon retiring and moving to San Francisco. That woman is dead now, and her husband, a terrifically grouchy man who once worked in the same department where Ella and the retiring man work now, is dead now, too.

"What are you going to do?" she says. "With all that extra time?"

"Play the piano," he says.

In a flash, Ella remembers her own father's retirement party, a terrible occasion on which a handful of his graduate students threw her father in the deep end of a swimming pool. The graduate students, you couldn't blame them, really, there's no way they could have known her father didn't know how to swim. *My watch isn't waterproof,* he screamed, but they didn't listen.

"They're giving you more books at the party," Ella says to the retiring man. "Act surprised."

"I know," the retiring man says. "I already heard."

Old West Night

I thought I might like to act in a Western, but it seemed to me there wasn't much left to say in a world in which "the West" was no longer wild, no longer empty, no longer fraught with possibility, not even the postmodern kind. A thousand stories all at once, destabilized subjectivity, an extra dose of danger: didn't some damned television show take care of all that when they visited the abandoned ghost town on their way to the Grand Canyon in the special one-hour episode somewhere near the series' last gasp? It seemed to me they did. So the literature of exhaustion was exhausted indeed, and I'd taken a job on a movie set. I'd been cast to play something like a hero, but behind the scenes, I'll admit, I was something else entirely.

My attention span had gone to hell. I couldn't memorize lines anymore, so it was a good thing the only lines I ever had were glimmers of wisdom like "I need a haircut," and "Will you please try my product?" That's right, I'm Lee Major (not to be confused with Lee Majors) the actor who portrayed the founder of the Flobee Retractable Hair Vacuum. I wasn't really that handsome, though; I guess I have the makeup to thank. I was *almost* that handsome; casting agents called me rugged. And I was a good bit older than I looked.

These days, I'm old enough to collect social security. Even back then I was probably too old to play the founder of the Flobee Retractable Hair Vacuum. For a good while, I've been old enough to play grandfathers, but once, in my late forties, I was actually cast to play a young newlywed lost on vacation in the Catskills. Does anyone even *go* to the Catskills anymore? The Catskills have become one of those places like Myrtle Beach and Mount Rushmore where the vacationers of yesteryear have taken up permanent residence, forever snapping photos with their Kodak Instamatics and sipping mai tais from plastic cups, their shadows crowding out the present-day masses, all of whom are too busy checking their smartphones to go anywhere at all. That's what I mean about my attention span; I, too, have taken to spending all day staring at my computer, waiting for someone else to eat an interesting lunch or otherwise brag about themselves. I know I'm not the only one who does this. It's one way to pass the time.

But I was lucky, back then, to be fresh-faced and small of stature. I played high school students well into my thirties. In spite of my pretty good track record scoring commercials and the occasional TV guest spot, I did not expect the call from my agent telling me I had a screen test for *Tumbleweed Town*, the latest Clint Eastwood vehicle, though Clint Eastwood had dropped out. From the first read-through up until the wrap party, everyone, and I do mean *everyone*, described the film in these exact terms: Clint Eastwood adapted the

screenplay from some out-of-the-way novel no one had
ever heard of; he wanted to direct and make a cameo
appearance as the sunburned sheriff, but he couldn't
get "the right people" signed on to play the other roles,
so he sold the script to someone else who, in turn, sold
it to a third someone else, who, in turn, put it through
about a million rewrites and changed the setting from
Arizona to Oklahoma. By that time, Clint was long
gone, but the memory of his sweat-stained shirts, his
figure casting a long shadow on the noonday street,
and the harsh white glare that made him squint into
the distance, all gave us a grasping sense of hope, or, if
not the prospect of fame and fortune, the promise of a
halfway decent paycheck for about six weeks running.

Something else Clint took with him was his money.
You've heard of doing a film on a shoestring? Well,
you might have called this doing a film on a G-string,
only there were no women in the cast. You know, the
great shoulder-rubbing masculinity of the trappers and
drummers and mineral prospectors of the west: it was
pretty wild, unbridled, you might say, full of tin pan
passion. Normally I'm not into that kind of thing, even
though I've been gay since before it was cool. And to be
fair, *Tumbleweed Town* was not what you would call por-
nographic; the producers wanted an R rating and an art
house following—sort of *Brokeback Mountain* meets *De-
liverance* meets *The Monkees,* because that's where I came
in: I could sing. And I don't mean I could merely carry
a tune; rather, I mean I had one hell of a set of pipes,
like I could have done opera, not that I liked to brag. I
know there are a lot of gay-seeming guys out there who

look good enough to put on a pair of chaps and make it believable, but how many of those same guys can sing "Don't Let the Train Whistle Wait" while riding bareback on an untrained pony? I was perfect for the role.

The second day of filming it started to rain. The clouds, when you could see them at all, were low and heavy, like fruit from a sagging branch. All morning, the puddles in the pasture grew large and deep, the whole world mired in mud. The director had permission to do some interior scenes in the living room of a local farmhouse, but all my scenes—I played the interloper—took place either on the town square set in the Tulsa studio or in the arid expanse of the great outdoors. Until the weather cleared up, I was free to do as I pleased.

Most of our downtime I spent alone in my trailer. Sometimes I read, sometimes I watched television with my laptop on the coffee table while I clicked the same listless links over and over again. I slept, showered, shaved, and microwaved, all the while wondering when and if someone would stop by to visit. The third rainy day in a row, someone did.

"Get the hell off my property," she said, once I'd opened the door to her furious pounding din. My windowpanes were still shaking when she said, "Hook up this jalopy to some Hollywood lim-o-zeen, and head on down the road."

"This is a state park," I said. "We have a permit."

She spit on the ground. "That's what I think of your permit," she said. "Who's in charge of this shit?"

Judging from her remarks you might have thought she was old, but she was young, about 25 at the time we first met. You might have thought she was tough, but she was gentle. You might have thought she was ugly, but she was beautiful. You might have thought, by now, I gave up being gay and fell in love with her, or she helped me rediscover my "true self," or she taught me the meaning of the land and the integrity of its people, or together, as in the finale for *Tumbleweed Town,* we roped cattle into a pen and then burst into song. None of that is true. What's true is that she was beautiful in an unconventional sense; she had so many freckles she might have looked like a leprosy case to the untrained eye, she had short, red hair she never combed, she smelled faintly of horses, I was not in love with her but came to love her. She, too, was gay, though her girlfriend worked on a Carnival Cruise ship and so was gone for months at a time, and that first day we met we spent all afternoon playing checkers and drinking these fancy cherry martinis she said her girlfriend had learned to make from Hillary Clinton herself, not on a Carnival Cruise ship but on Martha's Vineyard, where both she and her girlfriend had worked tending bar before cashing it all in and moving, for some inexplicable reason, to the open gash on the earth called Oklahoma.

Her name was Bonnie. "I own this piece of land," she said. This was after the shouted threats from the window, but before the checkers and martinis. "You can go down to City Hall and check."

"We have a producer," I said. "Maybe I should give one of his assistants a call."

"Shit," she said. "You can call him anything you want to."

"I call him Steve," I said. "His real name is Donald."

"You're funny," she said. "Asshole."

Bonnie did own the land, though not the whole stretch of it—the part where we'd set up shop was half hers and half on lease from the Osage Nation; just a couple of weeks after our departure it would become the construction site for a brand new casino. A few miles away, the oil and gas companies would set up shop and suck out the last drops of deadly money. I heard from some of the locals employed on set that Bonnie and her girlfriend ended up getting jobs at the blackjack tables at the casino, but they never sold their land. Her girlfriend was part Osage, but she looked, in photos, like she was white. It's hard to understand unless you've spent some time in Oklahoma.

I don't actually remember how it was that Bonnie and I made the transition from bitter antagonists to companionable checker players, but we spent all day every day together for two and a half weeks, exactly eighteen days and nights of nothing but driving rain and hard-whipping wind. Something like that had never before happened in the history of Oklahoma, and the floods came as an unwelcome surprise.

"It's a mud hole out here," I said, our fifth or sixth day together, as we tromped to the grocery store for mixers and chips. I stepped around the growing puddles while she splashed directly into their unfathomable expanse. She wore hip waders and a classic, yellow raincoat, the kind you see in children's books and old-fashioned movies. One thing I haven't mentioned is that she was taller than me, a lot taller.

"You have money?" she said. "Bring your wallet?"

"Sure," I said, because this was part of the bargain we had made: I paid for everything and she had all the local connections and good sense. I assumed she was broke and didn't ask why, a prudent decision I would realize later. But everyone was broke in Oklahoma, so she didn't stand out.

She took my wallet from me and pulled out three twenties and a ten. "For later," she said, stuffing the bills into the front pocket of her raincoat. I knew what she meant, since she had a cousin who sold pot out of the trunk of his car, and already we had become his best customers.

At the grocery store, she was judicious and I was rapacious, like a bear getting ready for winter. I wanted only junk food: Fritos and Cheetos and Twizzlers and Twix. She stocked up on lemons and limes and remembered the salt for rimming our glasses. She also had sense enough to pick up a bag of baby carrots and some frozen dinners, in case we wanted something more closely resembling actual food later on. All the clerks and even the manager seemed to know her, though they were not particularly friendly.

On the seventh day of rain, one of the other actors came over to ask to borrow my computer, to do his taxes, he said, which were long overdue. His name was Sherman, and he played the mayor of Tumbleweed Town, a bit part, but an important one insofar as the interloper (me) runs off with his wayward son. Sherman was a local, married with two grown kids. He and Bonnie seemed well-acquainted, somehow, though again, their relationship did not seem like a particularly warm one.

"This thing got a battery?" Sherman said, grabbing my laptop in a way that I thought was a little too rough.

"You have to plug it into the wall," I said. "Carefully."

"Power's out at my house," he said. "My wife's on vacation."

I knew that was my cue to invite him to make himself at home in my trailer, but I wasn't sure about his pot-smoking status, and I hated to interrupt the fun.

"And break out the bong," he said. "These taxes are a bitch." He looked at Bonnie and nodded. "Bonnie," he said. "Tell your folks I said hello."

I was a little afraid of Sherman. At my audition, he'd tried to scare me off by telling me my headshot looked like Liberace, and ever since then he'd committed other vaguely homophobic offenses, telling me I should comb my hair, asking if I'd ever joined the glee club in school, that kind of thing. Mostly I didn't let it bother me, but I could tell he had a mean streak none of us—except for maybe Bonnie—had seen on full display. Probably he'd been cast to play the mayor of Tumbleweed Town as a kind of payoff, a bargain between the film's producers and the local brute squad. Bonnie, though, had not been chosen for anything at all.

He put his feet up on my sofa without taking off his shoes. I watched as Bonnie stared at the mud caked on the soles of his work boots; she pointed at the sofa's cushions and looked at me meaningfully. Unwilling to challenge Sherman's implicit authority, I shrugged, poured Doritos into a bowl, and asked him if he'd heard when we might start shooting again.

"Not until the rain stops," he said. "Might as well get something done."

"Don't cheat on those taxes now," Bonnie said. "The Feds don't work for your kind no more."

He looked up from the laptop's screen, fumbled through the cushions for the television's remote control. "Smart," he said. "Our Bonnie always has something smart to say. What's two plus two, Bonnie, and don't stop to use your fingers."

"Don't forget the dickhead deduction," she said. "You'll make a million."

We went on like this for a while—Sherman monopolizing my laptop while Bonnie and I watched some sappy Lifetime movie on TV—when Bonnie had the idea we ought to go try to spot some bobcats down by the river.

"I don't like bobcats," I said. "And I'm quite sure bobcats don't like me."

"Ever seen one?" Sherman said. I knew then he was taking her side.

"What about the rain?" I said. "The riverbanks will be a mess."

"Lee don't want to melt," Bonnie said. "He's a little precious sometimes."

"No I'm not."

"Let's get one of them trick ponies," Sherman said. "So he don't have to get his feet wet."

Of course I had no choice but to agree to checking out the river on foot. To be clear, this was not the kind of river meant for rafting expeditions or fishing or really recreation of any kind. It was too small, too dirty, probably poisoned. The water was slow-moving and rusty, like the stagnant byproducts of some foul-smelling factory somewhere, like wastewater barely treated for parasites, like third-world water that would give you a disease. Bonnie said she and her sisters swam in it when they were kids, but she wouldn't touch it now. Sherman laughed and dipped a toe in, not a particularly brave act, but Bonnie and I were made to act impressed. The rain had slowed to a sprinkle now, and the sky, a sickly, yellow curtain flapping in the breeze, had lifted until it became a frame for the river's meandering malaise.

Bonnie pointed to a couple of scratches in the mud she said were bobcat tracks. Crouching on my haunches to get a better look, I saw what looked to me like rivulets from the river's continuous rushing and receding, little more than byproducts of a half-hearted flood. Sherman said Bonnie was right: just wait until dusk, he said. Watch for their yellow eyes.

We found a dry spot under a hulking river birch and Bonnie dumped the contents of her backpack onto a blanket she'd tucked under her arm. Neither Sherman nor I had thought to bring anything along except ourselves, but Bonnie came prepared with a shot glass, lime wedges presliced in a plastic bag meant to keep the morning newspaper dry in the driveway, a salt cellar she'd stolen from a local steakhouse called The Ranchers Club, and a bottle of Hornitos Reposado. She'd also brought along a pocketknife and some matches, though we decided, after some discussion, it was too wet for a fire.

When I look back on what happened to Bonnie, I don't know how anyone is supposed to make it in this world. I mean, she was tougher than anyone. If we *had* seen a bobcat that night, she would have been the one to know the right course of action, which, now that I think about it, probably would have been something along the lines of freeze and don't lock eyes with it or run like hell for the lights of the town. But we relaxed into the mosquito-covered sultriness of the evening, and Sherman, who was allowed to lean against the river birch because of his bad back, began to tell stories.

"First movie we made around here was a Western," he said. "And none of this musical theater crap, either." He looked at me. "No offense."

"None taken," I said. "It's a stupid idea for a script."

"I thought it was funny," Bonnie said. "It's supposed to be funny, right?"

"Anybody's guess," I said. "Probably it'll go straight to some website somewhere if they can't get it into a festival."

"The first movie was a *real* Western," Sherman said. "I got to shoot a gun."

"My daddy worked the props," Bonnie said. "I remember that gun."

I sucked on a lime wedge and turned to Sherman in what I thought was a knowing pose. "Did all the actors get paid?" I said.

"The money was good," he said. "Back then."

"My daddy worked for shit," Bonnie said. "His whole life."

Sherman launched into some song and dance about the value of the dollar, some version of which I'd heard only a couple of days before. It bugged me that Bonnie nodded at the especially dumb parts, like when he said the government had its big hand in our pockets and the fees you paid to get your driver's license and renew your plates were just taxes in disguise. He even said some shit about a new world order, one in which an international monetary system would replace the gold standard and we'd all be made to move into energy-efficient pods. Again, Bonnie nodded, and I pretended to be distracted by a dragonfly or brush blowing in the distance. The clouds threatened on the horizon just as the sun settled into a hazy hint of goodbye.

It was dark by the time we tromped back to my trailer. I tripped over some downed branches and so was bleeding, but not badly, from both elbows and knees. You could hardly see the scratches through all the splashes of mud. Bonnie called me Zombie-boy and Sherman offered to wet a paper towel, both signs I'd earned my merit badge out by the river. They were kind to me most of the time, but not kind to one another. Or, to speak of actual consequences, Sherman was not kind to Bonnie.

The next night, we all listened to loud music and danced until my trailer shook. Sherman was still working on his taxes, but wanted to take a break, a bunch of cheats he said, he needed some time to think. Bonnie had the big idea we should go shoot some pool at a bar called the Stonewall, a shithole weak-drink kind of place across the street from the college. The bar's owners favored Civil War decor over the pink triangle or rainbow flag, but everyone knew who was welcomed there, and I'd say that night it was probably more my crowd than Sherman's. Bonnie's crowd, too, maintained a notable presence, though they kept to themselves in a corner underneath the dartboards. Bonnie waved to some people who pointed knowingly to the television set, as if there were some shared history there, some secret knowledge. I asked her to introduce me.

"Nah," she said. "They're real nerdy."

I was surprised she thought I was either better-than-nerdy or worse, I wasn't sure which. "Come on," I said. "I want to meet some of your friends."

"Bonnie don't got no *friends*," Sherman said. "Only what I'd call *cohorts*."

Now with something to prove, Bonnie pushed Sherman aside, grabbed my hand, and strode toward the laughing women by the dartboards. Closer now, I realized she was right; they *were* nerdy, but in an easy, comfortable way. I found out all four of them were entomologists at the university, each one obsessed with a different insect I'd never heard of. Bonnie acted as if all of this were old news, another reason why she more often kept to herself. It was clear she did not want Sherman to join us, but he did anyway.

"You girls better get home," he said. "It's getting late."

"Mind your own, Sherman," Bonnie said. By now she'd ordered a pitcher of beer and consumed most of it herself. Not to be outdone, Sherman had started drinking boilermakers, a college boy's drink, he said, but worth the price of admission. I thought a game of darts or pool might settle everyone's nerves and so suggested "a bit of sport," as I called it, much to everyone's laughter. I realized then I was the nerdy one, the friend who stood out. Bonnie was not ashamed of me, though she could have been. She settled into a booth between two of the entomologists, pulled out a cigarette, and slapped two greasy dollar bills on the table.

"I don't smoke," she said. "Unless I'm at a bar."

"What about the baby?" Sherman said. "You're gonna kill that baby."

It had never occurred to me that Bonnie could be pregnant, and it turned out she wasn't, not anymore anyway. I'd seen photos of her girlfriend and neither she nor Bonnie seemed like the type to want to set up shop in the gay lifestyle section, all trendy and outfitted in matching jumpsuits to protect themselves against bigotry, driving to Tulsa for fertility treatments and reading storybooks called *My Two Moms*. They didn't have enough money, for one thing, and they didn't seem to go in for the latest and greatest in family values. I knew the girlfriend had been married once before, to a man, and maybe there were a couple of kids somewhere. But Bonnie? Pregnant? No way.

Bonnie kicked the booth and the entomologists grabbed their glasses, watching as the various brownish liquids inside sloshed and almost spilled. "Stay out of it, Sherman," she said.

"He's real sorry," Sherman said. "Wants to make it up to you."

She looked at him and did something strangely tender: she touched his hand. "Stop while you're ahead, Sherman," she said. "Lee don't need to know."

Sherman turned to me in the booth. "You didn't know?" he said. "Bonnie likes to swing both ways."

He looked back at Bonnie with a watery, focused

eye, as if he had other, more mysterious ways to hurt her none of us yet knew. We'd all been drinking like drowning fish for days, so he must have had something specific in mind, to admonish her like that in public. It annoyed me, strangely, to think Sherman knew more about Bonnie's history than I did.

It was still raining when we left the bar, a plastic statue of Stonewall Jackson himself waving us goodbye. Both Bonnie and Sherman were trashed, but I imagined myself sober. "Hey, mister," Bonnie said, as we staggered the two and a half miles back to my trailer. "Aren't you the inventor of the Flobee Retractable Hair Vacuum?" She liked to tease me that way, and I let her. Still, I was worried, like maybe I should have been carrying her or at least offering her my much-warmer jacket. Sherman made a point to walk at least two steps ahead of us, and he had a flashlight on his key chain he refused to use. As we stepped over downed branches and hopped curbs for a shortcut, I felt buoyant, like a teenager in a movie. One thing I still love about being an actor is that you can do things like this—hang out with people you otherwise never would have had reason to speak to, assume an instant camaraderie, say stuff like *I'll be there with bells on* and mean it—and come away as if the whole thing were the proverbial midsummer night's dream. I felt very close to Bonnie those two and a half weeks, but I haven't spoken to her since.

Our final act of derring-do was to host a cast party in my trailer. It was still raining, and by then there was a rumor going around the director had lost his funding, or most of it, at least, the part that was going to keep the catering table stocked and our paychecks arriving on time. No one had anything else lined up, so we stuck around, eager, in some pathetic way, to see our names in the closing credits and hope some casting agent somewhere would single us out for some unnamed future attention. Depending on the particular project and the mix of people involved, most parties of this particular nature took place after everything had wrapped, but the rain made everything feel slippery, delirious somehow, like all of us had become vaudeville performers from another era, desperate, as we were, for one last chance to live up to the promise of living life outside the company man's walls. The money was always terrible, but we made up for it in other ways.

Bonnie had bought some cactus Christmas lights from the dollar store and I'd Xeroxed copies of our director's headshot, doodled mustaches and eyeglasses and devil's horns all over them, and Scotch-taped them around the trailer in what I thought were funny places— above the toilet, on the ice bucket, around the edges of my cheap chandelier. Sherman made something he called his wife's famous artichoke cheese dip, and the whole thing started to assume some greater importance, as if Clint Eastwood himself had brought us all together for one final shebang. Bonnie wanted to play cowboy music, to go with the theme, she said, but I nixed the idea in favor of the classic rock channel on my satellite TV. We'd invited everyone we could think of, told them all to bring a guest, and, as a result, decided the party would be both an indoor *and* outdoor affair. Bonnie borrowed some lawn chairs from her cousin and lined them up like audience seats in a tent revival alongside the long end of my trailer. We set up a tarp to keep off the rain.

More people showed up than I might have liked. It's supposed to seem festive, somehow, when strangers crash your party, but I was beginning to feel nervous when the artichoke cheese dip ran out and some guy brought out a guitar and not just played it but also plugged it in. A little music goes a long way inside one of those trailers, and I found myself shouting to be heard. Even worse, people were using my back bedroom to smoke pot, which would have been fine, really, had anyone thought to make room enough to invite me in. The hallway between the bathroom and the bedroom had become congested to the point of suffocation, though there was a strange sense of order and symmetry: the same people, in the exact same formation, kept going in and out of the bathroom at regular intervals. One of them I recognized as Bonnie's cousin, though I hadn't seen Bonnie in a while.

Sherman approached me from behind, clapped his hand on my shoulder. "The rain finally stopped," he said. "Can you hear the coyotes?"

"Are you kidding me?" I said, motioning to the party's merriment. I didn't feel too merry. "Not with these people around."

"Step outside a bit," he said. "They're howling at the moon out there. It's really something to hear."

I told him I needed to pee first, but above the party's din he might have thought I was saying my own name. "Of course I'll talk to Lee first," he said. "You're the one who owns this place."

"Never mind," I shouted. "I'll meet you out back."

But when I made my way to the bathroom, Sherman was following me, and not in an idle way, either. When I took a step, he took a step. When I stopped to scoot around some unsuspecting guest or piece of furniture, he did the same. I tried to throw him off my trail by hopping over the coffee table, but he anticipated my every move, darting through conversation clusters and dodging a pile of muddy shoes by the door. Something about the way he was acting reminded me of a scene from *Tumbleweed Town*, one of the few scenes we'd already shot. The mayor (Sherman) hangs up a Wanted poster with my picture on it, and when he (seemingly by accident) drives a nail through my forehead as he hammers the poster to a tree, everyone laughs. Everyone except the mayor, that is, because he's busy plotting his next move.

Almost to the bathroom now, I turned to him and spoke directly into his ear. "I'll just be a minute, Sherman," I said. "Jeez."

"Don't go in there," he said. "I'm telling you."

Bonnie's cousin was a tall guy, taller than Sherman and definitely taller than me. He wore a muscle-shirt advertising beer and blue jeans that had been cut off at the knees. And he was much older than Bonnie, I figured, probably almost my age, though he never talked about a wife or a family and he seemed to live more or less out of his car, couch-surfing sometimes, waiting around for another oil rig job out in the Gulf. I didn't trust him, but I didn't know him very well, either, so somehow I was stupid enough to be surprised when I saw him with a gun.

Theatrical and cinematic simulations aside, I had never been around someone with a real gun. I mean never. Growing up, my family was more the gatherer type, and, even when I lived in the worst parts of the worst cities, I'd never seen reason for self-protection. So I was unnerved to see him there, sitting cross-legged on the edge of the bathtub, a shotgun slung over his lap.

Another man I didn't recognize pushed the door closed against my body before I could step all the way into the bathroom-proper. I could tell the man was stronger than me, so when the force of his heaving shoulder sent me back into the crowded hallway, I did not try to push the door open again. But I should have. That's the whole reason I've been telling this story—because I should have. When I've told different versions of this story on other occasions, I've included the details about Bonnie's cousin, the muscle-shirt he was wearing, the shotgun, my city-slicker's naivety when I came into such close contact with unanticipated firearms. I've also included the detail about the other man shoving me out of the bathroom before I could get a good look at what was going on in there. But the part I always leave out is that Bonnie was in there, with a third man, and the third man had his pants down, though Bonnie was fully clothed.

"Come on now, Lee," Sherman said. For some inexplicable reason, he put his hand—a ghostly white against the fake wood of the trailer's walls—on the light switch and turned off the light in the hallway. We stood there in the dark, a crowd of sweaty, beer-soaked actors and townies and townie-actors, slick and sick with the knowledge something terrible was happening there in the bathroom, though no one had the guts to do anything about it.

"You want to hear some coyotes?"

"Yeah," I said. "Let's go."

And though I saw her again the next day and we partied like hell and laughed our asses off about what a crazy night we'd had, I did something I'll always regret, which is to say I left Bonnie there in the bathroom. I left her there and went out into the Old West night, as if her suffering were a TV show and I her distracted viewer, ready, as I always was, to change the channel.

The Dot

My twin brother suffers from premature hair loss. Refusing all topical creams, dyes, drugs, or implants, Aaron motors around our prosperous neighborhood with the confidence of the newly divorced. He drives a convertible, one of those high-end brands with X or Z as a suffix. He's not actually divorced, though, he's married to a woman ten years his senior, a computer programmer who, in spite of staying away from conditioner, hairspray, gel, or mousse, has the kind of curly, brown hair you might mistake for a movie star's. Her trademark, Aaron says, without irony. He's right: she's beautiful.

They make a fine couple, though people are always asking why such a gorgeous woman would marry a toad like him. The same is true about my own marriage, I suppose, except in our case I am the toad and my husband is the princess. My brother's hair loss, though, draws attention to his other flaws and for that reason I admire its shiny grandeur. Were it not for that sunburned patch of skin I know I would want to kill him for sure.

We're late, my husband said one morning before we were supposed to go over to my brother's house for brunch. My husband, always concerned about potential tardiness, taught sixth grade at the same middle school where I'm paid about two cents an hour to keep the DVD players in good repair and occasionally order science videos from The Discovery Channel catalog. Like most American History teachers, my husband did double duty not just as the coach of the peewee football team but also as the sponsor of the Academic Quiz Bowl Squad. Sometimes he left his stopwatch hanging around his neck even after we'd gone to bed for the night.

We're not late, I told him. And what if we were? No one's going to send us to the principal's office.

I don't like to be late, he said, hurling my purse across the room as if it were an errant catcher's mask in an otherwise immaculate equipment room. I like my waffles hot, he said, and before I could collect the spilled contents of my purse he was out the front door.

I reached under the couch to retrieve a lipstick tube and wondered again why I bothered with makeup. All the kids at school called me The Owl. I didn't know what they called my husband, but I suspected they'd assigned him a considerably more flattering nickname. Always Mr. Cool Guy, my husband—Chet is his name, short for Chester—was fond of telling jokes like the following: *How do you break a sixth-grader's finger? Answer: You punch him in the nose.* For this, the seventh-graders thought him some kind of god.

I fumbled with some loose change under the rocking chair and finally arranged myself for a more relaxed departure. Aaron and Faye lived only two doors down, so one might have imagined we enjoyed the kind of relationship where borrowing a cup of sugar or a step-ladder was common as the morning paper. Not so. Tension replaced our usual neighborly merriment as soon as Aaron graduated from dental school and started losing his hair. Imagining themselves older and richer than their boring old sister and brother-in-law, Aaron and Faye started running with a more sophisticated crowd. Now they're talking about replacing their Formica countertops with granite, building a gazebo in the backyard, and eventually, having children. Chet and I could never compete.

Well, I figured at least one of us should be on time, Chet whispered as I slid into the chair beside him. Shouldn't you be wearing more makeup?

Oh, come on, I said. What are you afraid of?

He was afraid of looking like a dork. All attempts at swaggering in front of middle-schoolers aside, my husband pretty much was a dork, and if I was honest with myself I had to admit his slow-wittedness was one of the reasons I decided to marry him in the first place. Lately I was sorry I did.

I hope you're ready for some fresh melon, Faye said from the kitchen.

Oh, you bet we are, Chet said. Really hits the spot.

Aaron brought in a basket of sweet rolls and Chet said, Oh, we just love sweet rolls. The other day Sylvia ate almost a whole roll of those cinnamon rolls in a tube. She leaves off the frosting, though, says it's too sweet. Don't you honey?

Chet loves sweet rolls, I said.

That's just the problem, Aaron said. Too many people

love sweet rolls. Not you two, of course, but the kids! Christ, if I've done one filling I've done a thousand.

Faye put Aaron through dental school by working two jobs doing tech support by day and web design by night, but he didn't appreciate her as much as he should have. Cynicism along with a strange, small-town nostalgia united Aaron and me. Together we were like matching broken-down tractors in a space-age economy. Most twins find creative ways to depart from the personality traits of their siblings, but our entire lives Aaron and I had been the same. I was not the wild one; neither was he the smart one. Born of ugly but overeducated parents, Aaron and I were co-valedictorians in high school, but finished last and next to last respectively in the same torturous track meets. We went to the same college where we both double-majored in Biology and Classics. He eventually married Faye in the same city park where I married my husband. His job, as it turned out, paid him a lot more money than mine paid me. His bald spot, though, gave me an odd sort of pleasure I could only describe as something like laughing gas. You didn't want to laugh, exactly, but crying, too, seemed out of the question.

How's the team? Aaron asked Chet. Quarterback learn how to throw yet?

Oh, these kids are runners, Chet said. Fast.

They spent a few minutes on the intricacies of first downs and field goals while I stared hard at my sweet roll.

Aaron winked at me and said, Good fan base, though, right? A great clamor at touchdown time? I'm sure your wife is full of, you know, pep?

Aaron knew the collapse of the Middle School Pep Club came as a result of my shifting my extracurricular allegiance away from athletics and toward the Science Club and Student Council. Wearing a rain poncho and waving a pompom every Friday night wasn't exactly my idea of a good time. Never afraid to exploit existing tensions between my husband and me, Aaron went on to cup his hands over his mouth and make the pretend sound of a roaring crowd.

We don't need a Pep Club, anyway, Chet said. We have a mascot. And a cheerleading squad. Last week, we had confetti shooting out of a cannon.

Faye came in from the kitchen and said, I caught the first quarter on the cable access channel. The confetti looked more like snowflakes, but then I guess the picture wasn't very good. You ought to see our new entertainment system in the basement. Who wants coffee?

I'll help, I said, standing. Let's go.

She followed me into the kitchen and said maybe they should make their own coffee.

Aaron doesn't drink coffee anymore, Faye said. I suppose Chet drinks decaf these days?

Tea, I said, embarrassed. I'll bring him some hot water.

Faye plugged in the waffle iron and stirred batter in a bowl. All these years and I never thought of her as the hostess type. For the sake of Aaron and his career, she sometimes pretended to care about wifely duties. Like me, she never imagined twenty-first century marriage demanded public appearances accompanied by adoring gazes at her husband, but she played the game as well as anyone.

Aaron and I have an announcement, she said, dropping crushed pecans into the batter.

Oh no, I said. Are you sure?

Not that, she said. Not yet.

I fiddled with a stack of coffee filters and said, Good. Everything all right?

Oh yeah, we're just doing some more remodeling, that's all. Aaron's putting in a hot tub. They're knocking out a wall.

They have to knock out a wall to put in a hot tub?

It's big enough for four, she said. They're breaking ground tomorrow morning.

You're welcome at our house, I said, immediately sorry I did. While the wall's knocked out and everything.

Faye poured batter into the waffle iron and told me about Aaron's plan to expand his dental practice. Teeth whiteners and implants, she said, were big business these days. The two of them would sleep in Aaron's office during the renovation. The dental office had a fully equipped kitchen and executive washroom, she said. And besides, they needed access to a computer.

Chet and I have a computer, I said.

Oh, we need a fast computer, she said. Aaron's website and everything.

I'd never really looked at Aaron's website, but I imagined a rotating gleaming white molar on a royal blue background. Maybe his photograph in the middle.

Of course, I said. But if you want to come over for dinner or something—

Faye finished a platter of waffles and we joined the

husbands in the dining room. They were in the middle of a conversation and didn't notice our arrival.

But I don't believe in multinational corporations, Chet said, his eyes squeezing shut and his lips sucking at a spoonful of fruit.

Aaron said, No one really believes in multinational corporations. They believe in the money. That's all. Can't you get behind a simple idea like that?

It's not so simple, my husband said. Oh good, the waffles are here.

Aaron said, Look Chet, I'm just like you, okay? I don't use pesticides on my lawn, I give to Habitat for Humanity, and I vote for the Democrats. So what's the big deal? I want my children to have a viable future, that's all.

You don't have any children, I said.

That's true, Faye said. We don't.

Aaron grabbed two waffles from the platter and said, Oh, and I suppose we all should stop brushing our teeth just because we don't have any cavities.

I'm getting false teeth, I said. Like George Washington's.

Aaron reached across my place for the butter. Fine, Sylvia, he said. Keep on being irresponsible. Go team.

My husband complimented Faye on the waffles and everyone ate in silence for a while. I tried not to think of the insides of our mouths, our tongues flattening against our gums, our incisors encrusted with syrup. My husband and I played these little dinner-party games with Aaron and Faye on a fairly regular basis, but we weren't really friends. We were consumers who shared the same demographics.

Chet and I just bought new bed linens, I said. Four hundred thread count sheets.

Chet started in on the magic of memory foam mattresses and Aaron nodded. Faye brought in another platter of waffles.

Feather pillows are too hard on Chet's allergies, I said, but before I could give my speech on synthetic fibers, I felt a sudden sharpness against one of my back teeth.

Faye said, What's the matter? Oh shit, your tooth. Oh god, there was a pecan shell in the waffle batter, Aaron, do something.

I said I was fine, and Faye fussed over me for a while. I watched as Chet drowned himself in orange juice. Later, Aaron brought out the blueprints for the new hot tub. We all pretended to be impressed with the underground heating system, our grunts and murmurs meant to signal appreciation for his technical expertise. Aaron leaned his chair back from the table and, in an instant, almost lost his balance. I resisted the urge to push him to the floor, but managed to sound concerned when he said he felt a little light-headed from eating too much. Before long I gave Chet the signal for an early departure. We made plans for them to attend the middle-school football game the following Friday.

Later that night my gums began to bleed.

Tie it to a doorknob, Chet said, doing yoga in front of the late night news. Or make yourself an ice pack from the freezer.

I've done all that, I said. Not the doorknob. But the ice pack didn't help.

We agreed I should call Aaron in the morning and arrange for some X-rays.

Aaron will know what to do, my husband said. He always does.

That's just the problem, I said. I squirted toothpaste on my finger.

Use a toothbrush, my husband said. Does a better job. You know I think Aaron's a bright guy? He's always annoyed me a little, but I think he means well.

I told him I couldn't use a toothbrush; the bristles provoked my bleeding gums. But Chet believed in the power of household appliances. Earlier that day, I had been grateful he didn't ask to see the warranty on Aaron's new big-screen TV. When Aaron and Faye purchased their new deep freeze, Chet brought his camera into the garage and took not just one photo of it, but an entire series from multiple angles. Once, when Aaron and Faye were first married, he spent so much time reading the instruction booklet that came with their food processor, Faye offered to let him take it home.

You can use my electric toothbrush, he said.

No thanks, I said. I'll find time for Aaron to look at it sometime tomorrow.

He rose from the downward dog and dove into bed, his arms outstretched in front of him as if he were some kind of disabled superhero. I tried again to brush my teeth with my finger, but gave up and came to bed.

He said, We could do it, you know. We could beat them.

We already beat them at backgammon and bridge, I said. What's left?

No, I mean we could really show 'em up.

I don't want to have a baby.

He buried his head underneath one of the pillows. I heard his muffled voice say, How did you know that's what I was going to say?

I always know, I said, and he seemed to accept the finality of the day's events. I knew Chet didn't want a baby as much as he wanted another member of his fan club, a football-sized human to toss around at PTA meetings. When my job as middle-school media specialist finally sent me over the edge, I wanted to go to graduate school. I didn't want to be pregnant while writing term papers and the last thing I needed was mandatory diaper change at exam time. Doubtless my husband would decorate the child with the school colors and carry it around on his shoulders, but I knew I would be left with the dirty work. For these and many other reasons, I always insisted on birth control.

Don't talk to me, he said, still underneath his hypoallergenic pillow. I'm tired.

I know, I said.

I didn't talk to him all that night and into the next morning. When we pulled our separate cars into the middle school's parking lot, I saw him fixing his hair in the rearview mirror of his practical sedan. We didn't speak as we walked in the double doors and past the principal's office. When he stopped in front of the gym, I told him I was going to Aaron's office right after school.

The tooth, I said. Maybe he can fix it.

I'll fix myself some soup, he said. For an after-school snack.

I spent most of the morning alphabetizing *Reading Rainbow* episodes in the library. At lunch, I did not, as I usually do, make my way to the coaches' table in the teachers' lounge. After school, I skipped my usual admiring glance through the window of the weight room and headed straight for the parking lot.

The exterior of Aaron's dental office always impressed me with its silver chromed street lamps and its lush tropical lawn care. Next door was a plastic surgeon and across the street a whole row of chiropractors, their wooden signs advertising a false quaintness in an otherwise neon-glowed commercial district. Aaron's regular patients had cleared out for the day by the time I walked into the lobby. I held my jaw firm against my open hand.

Aaron sat on top of the reception counter looking over what looked like a page from the *Wall Street Journal.* Poised in his right hand was a yellow highlighter marker.

You're such a wimp, Sylvia, he said without looking up. Faye's in Exam One. She'll get you started.

I passed a poster of the Mormon Tabernacle Choir holding up their toothbrushes as if they were a thousand torches on a thousand Statues of Liberty. *Brush,* the poster read. *Because God Demands It.*

So I guess we're going to do it, Faye said, attaching a spit bib to the collar of my shirt. Start trying, I mean.

Good thing twins run in the family. One for Aaron and one for me.

It was as if she had spent the day talking on the phone with Chet, together, their devious minds spreading something like tooth decay to every hungry mouth in America. I knew what would happen next. Aaron and Faye would have a baby or maybe two (and I would be expected to throw a baby shower), followed by a christening at the Presbyterian Church, preschool at the skyscraper with the monkey bars out front, an impressive career as a spelling bee champ, and finally, my sweet-cheeked niece and/or my dashing young nephew would start high school and either play football or become the captain of the cheerleading squad, my husband's graying cotton-ball sideburns still standing watch over the sidelines.

No way, I decided. My husband and I would move before I would let myself become Auntie Owl. Or maybe we would get a divorce and I would move. In any case I would find a way to make Aaron suffer for his upper-middle-class bliss. No way he should play lord of the manor while I wasted away in film projector land.

Fix the tooth, I told Aaron when he came in from the lobby. And don't talk to me.

I guess you heard our big news then, Aaron said. One thing about genetics, any child of mine will look a lot like you.

I don't believe it, I said. You're calling me ugly. You're calling me ugly to my face. Well you're ugly, I said. You have acne scars that would make models faint.

I'm not calling you ugly, he said. I'm calling you

crazy. If I called you ugly I guess I'd be calling myself ugly, too, then. You're pretty, Sylvia, you're just not very—refined. Aaron poked at my sore tooth with a sharp instrument. He asked me if it hurt and I said yes.

No problem, he said. We'll make an appointment for a crown. Until then I'll give you some codeine.

By this time, I found myself fantasizing about using one of Aaron's fancy gold-plated drills to bore a hole through the roof of his mouth. I didn't want him calling me hysterical, though, so I acted casual.

Construction started today, I said. On the hot tub?

Oh yeah, he said. They knocked out the bedroom wall. I guess Faye told you we're sleeping here tonight.

Yeah, I said. My gums feel better. Thanks.

I'll put it on your tab, he said. He laughed. That funny twin brother. That funny, smart, successful twin brother. I longed for him to spend just one minute feeling as useless as I did on a regular basis. My fingers closed around my car keys, but I could not remember which one started the car and which one opened the trunk. Leaving the dental office should not have seemed like such a chore. Maybe I wouldn't leave at all. The time was ripe for action.

Aaron and Faye stood over a carton of dental floss and waved me off. They must have thought me little more than a grateful twin sister with a toothy grin. Little did they know I was right then formulating my plans.

We'll see you at the big game, Aaron said. Rah rah.

Pretending to exit the lobby, I instead ducked into a broom closet in the marble-floored entryway. I sat on an overturned mop bucket and waited.

She's jealous, I heard Aaron say to Faye. I think Chet's sperm are blanks or something.

His remarks only hardened my resolve. I waited in the broom closet a long time. Knowing my husband would be worried, I considered sending him a text, but eventually decided to make him wait. I heard Aaron and Faye going over figures from the *Wall Street Journal*. They messed around with the dental office website, debating at length whether or not they should run a discount on root canals. Finally I heard them go to bed.

After I was sure they had been asleep for at least thirty minutes, I crept out of my hiding place in the broom closet and retrieved a yellow highlighter marker from behind the reception counter. I took off my shoes and passed through the executive washroom and into the fully equipped break room. The foldout couch tilted at an angle, and light from the streetlamps shone through a window. Aaron slept with his arms tight around Faye's shoulders.

After uncapping the highlighter marker and inhaling its slightly toxic scent, I drew one little dot on the top of Aaron's bald head. The dot seemed to me a great idea, an embryo that would grow into an entire planet, an asteroid, a sun. I made the dot bigger and Aaron took a swat in my general direction. Relieved he still had his eyes closed, I made the dot bigger still. Now the dot was the size of a saucer. I imagined Aaron going to one of my husband's football games, his head like a great misshapen loaf of bread rising from the back row of the stadium. I made the dot even larger, long lines of buttery goodness flowing down toward Aaron's ears.

Now the dot was the size of a dinner plate and Faye was beginning to stir. I walked out of the break room and the dot stared at me from its crowning glory on the top of Aaron's head. Worried they might hear me unlock the front door, I slipped back into the broom closet, curled up in a corner, and rested my head on a pile of dust rags. Again I decided not to call or text my husband. Eventually I would go home. For a few minutes, though, I sat there listening to Aaron snore. When we were old—toothless and gray—he would garner great respect and I would draw looks of disgust from schoolchildren passing me on the street. For tonight, at least, I had evened the score.

You were gone for a long time, Chet said when I walked in the front door. What were you doing?

Nothing, I said.

Nothing?

Nothing important, I said. I mean, nothing that anyone would ever notice.

He seemed content with my feeble explanation for my whereabouts, and nothing happened for a while. Chet didn't win any football games. My tooth didn't get any better. The hole in Aaron's and Faye's backyard never became a hot tub, and in its place they poured another concrete block and added an extra room for the baby's nursery. I sent them a handmade card when their son arrived. On the cover I drew a smiley face—a big, toothy grin, a wrinkled nose that looked like a raisin, and two hard, mean dots, for the eyes.

Recipe for Disaster

I'm just her aunt, so I suppose I should not have minded when she made a fool of herself on national television. Twenty-one years later, and still, I remember every detail of the day she was born—the balloons floating up toward the acoustic tiles on the waiting room's ceiling, the simultaneous explosion of a thousand flashbulbs, the burnt bacon scent of the burgers brought in from across the street. When your only sister gives birth to her only child, you want to be there for her, maybe especially if you've never had any children of your own. That's right, I'm a walking cliché—the spinster aunt. I've been single my entire adult life, and I have no shame. Nieces and nephews, however, take on greater importance for those of us who never married. My niece, long before her fifteen minutes of fame, came to visit every now and then and earned a place of some prominence in my will.

She's a beautiful girl, really. My sister and her husband moved to Florida shortly after she was born, so she was lucky that way—to escape Oklahoma. Ten years ago, my sister was killed in a freak accident; a single-engine Cessna crashed into her house. Her husband was at work at the time, and my niece, perky and perfect in a plaid skirt and Mickey Mouse ears, was on a field trip to Walt Disney World with her seventh-grade class. Even without her mother, my niece was better off in the sunshine state, though the barren red soil in Oklahoma might have given her some much-needed humility. I still live in Oklahoma, of course. I have a garden, two pit bulls, three cats, and a horse I sometimes ride at a boarding facility a few miles down the road. I used to have chickens and two giant tortoises, but really, I'm not your typical hard-edged, wind-whipped Oklahoma churchgoer. I don't go to church, which can get you in a lot of trouble around here if you're not careful. My niece never went to church either, or at least I didn't think she did. No matter. Never one to miss an opportunity, she perfected the church-going script.

A better script would have been helpful that night on television, the night of her downfall, but no one asked me. I watched the pageant live, just like everyone else did. And I was rooting for her. I had a few friends over; we made mixed drinks and microwaved popcorn and decorated the living room. My own niece almost became Miss America, which was kind of a joke, really, among my friends. Aunt America, they called me in e-mail messages. Aunt Sally. Aunt Florida.

So when people starting calling her a bitch on all those entertainment news shows I felt bad on her behalf. Okay, I took her out of my will. Later, I felt guilty. And I couldn't stand all those queens on television acting oh-so-shocked about a few semi-nude photos; I mean, really, those horny little punks? I put her back in the will for a while until she came to Oklahoma to visit. She insulted me, not on purpose, and I took her back out again. Once she was fired from her Miss Florida job, I sold my giant tortoises, added the profits to my savings account, and started a family trust. My lawyer, also my next-door neighbor and the school district's only bus driver, is getting tired of hearing from me.

Okay, so I'm gay. I don't generally talk like that—*I'm gay*. And people in this town don't use the word "lesbian" unless they're recounting events from a television show or badmouthing the university two towns over. But if you want to get technical about it, sure, I am one. My long-time partner and I live in relative harmony and have for many years. I dislike the word "partner," however, due to its square-dancing connotations. What's the official state dance of Oklahoma? You guessed it, the square dance. What do I call her, instead? My sweetie. When various bureaucratic institutions ask if I'm married or single, though, I call myself single, and so does Meredith. Our tax returns do not lie. You could say we're old-fashioned and/or closeted, but really, we're just being truthful. Gay marriage in Oklahoma? That'll be the day.

My niece is pretty famous by now, in a sideshow kind of way. Her name is Caitlin Loi—"rhymes with joy," as she said in a less-aired part of her pageant interview. She's been doing pageants since she was fourteen; my sister, I'm sure, is rolling over in her grave. Not that my sister especially cared about feminist issues—she didn't; she left that to me—but she was big into academic achievement and always swore she wouldn't allow Caitlin to start dating until she was thirty. She was making a joke, of course, but I know for a fact she would not have approved of David's new group of friends, the most troubling of whom is a certain sleazy Mr. pony-tailed "bring your bathing suit" photographer named William Hamburger. That's William Hamburger of Hamburger Photography, Wellington, West Palm: Digital Proofs and a Whole Lotta Beef.

David changed after my sister died. Not a surprise, I guess, since most men change anyway, whether their wives turn up dead or not. But he *really* changed. Once a workaholic powerhouse engineer for NASA, he took early retirement and became a surfer, the kind who never surfed, but instead showed up drunk every night at the Hard Rock Cafe and told every woman at the bar she had pretty hair. I mean, come on. Not every woman has pretty hair.

After the pageant and the ensuing fallout, David and Caitlin were coming to visit. David's more or less an idiot, but he's no homophobe, so I think he was hoping a visit to our house would remind Caitlin of her gay roots or something. So, Meredith—who really was a good sport about all this—and I were cleaning the house in preparation for a visit from my bigoted niece and her pushy father when someone had the bright idea to watch the pageant interview again on YouTube—a joke, I guess, to remind us of our brush with fame. Meredith does tech support for a living, so she can do all kinds of fancy things on a computer like put George W. Bush's head on Oprah's body and get the Jonas Brothers to sing their songs backwards and make the lyrics sound like "Satan wants my sandwich." So, we had

Meredith's laptop out on the front porch—the two of us together in an oversized Adirondack chair—and the YouTube clip was just getting to the part where Caitlin says, "no offense to anyone out there,"—anyone? How about your dead mother's only sister?—"but I believe marriage should be between a man and a woman," when David and the bigot herself pulled up in our driveway.

"Turn it off," I said. "Pretend you're playing solitaire."

"Come on," Meredith said. "Like she hasn't seen it a thousand times before." She hit play and started the interview again from the beginning. But by the time David and Caitlin heaved their suitcases out of the trunk and released Caitlin's dog from a crate in the back seat, Caitlin's controversial interview was long over and we were laughing our asses off at Miss Idaho's lament for the lost potato. But really, the pageants are a racket. They're practically prehistoric by now; who *does* that kind of thing these days? (Unfortunately, people say the same thing about going to the public library, my place of employment.) But watching these modern-day minstrel shows always makes me feel at least a little sorry for all the young women—not just my niece. I mean, they're fools to believe in the lie. When I realized something I'd said earlier—"she's a beautiful girl"—was the same thing that asshole Donald Trump said about her during the dark days immediately after the pageant, I felt sorry for her all over again.

So, like I said, you worry on behalf of these beautiful young women right up until the moment they show their contempt for older, unmarried women for taking the high road, a road so high the young women don't even *know* it's the high road, they don't even know it's a road, in fact, they just think you're some dumb old lady. I know this kind of thing is controversial these days, but my decision to live with Meredith was not a biological one. I made a conscious, deliberate decision to ditch men— partly for political reasons and partly because of plain old love—and she did the same. Meredith is beautiful enough to have been in pageants, but I am not. This is neither mere flattery nor self-deprecation on my part; she had many boyfriends and one fairly handsome (but brutal) husband before she met me; whereas I had only my nerdy friends at the library and a very large bill from the orthodontist. My teeth are pretty straight these days, and we both jog, but still, she is the beauty of the family.

Anyway, hers was the more difficult decision, the braver one. In my case, choosing to spend my life with a woman was easy. The pageants didn't want me, so I didn't want them either. Not that David and Caitlin have the first clue about any of this. In spite of Caitlin's professed bigotry, they love Meredith. Caitlin calls Meredith "auntie" and always has, and David often sends her funny forwarded e-mails about politics or cooking. Willing spokespeople for the zeitgeist, David and Caitlin always assumed ours was a romance fated by the stars, a predetermined biological fact, the only possible outcome since the day each of us was born. And for our parts, Meredith and I have always indulged them in these fantasies; the whole thing seemed too complicated to explain, and besides, we're private people, inclined to taking pleasure in one another and our pets and to spending Saturday nights at home.

So, the YouTube clip of the pageant was nearing its closing credits when Caitlin's dog began to bark. You might expect someone like Caitlin to have a high-pitched yapper carried around in a fuzzy handbag—her dog *looks like* he would be a high-pitched yapper and he's small enough for the handbag routine—but the noise coming from the Chihuahua/Terrier cross never fails to instill fear in the hearts of the weak-minded. Mayonnaise is his name, a terrible name for a dog. Mayonnaise, the little punk, has a bark like a hundred-pound Doberman's.

"Hi, Mayonnaise," I said before greeting either David or Caitlin. I guess you could call this passive-aggressive.

Meredith asked about the traffic; Caitlin smiled weakly. David, normally full of boyish athleticism, carried himself with heaviness and dread—his mustache had returned, and he'd put on weight. Prednisone, I suspected, or too many corn dogs. Also, he wore a pinkie ring and a thin leather strap tied around his wrist—both looked like low-dollar trinkets he'd picked up at the cash register in some head shop somewhere. I repeated my greeting to Mayonnaise and tried not to look at either one of the humans. Meredith, undaunted, ignored the dog and seemed sincere when she said she was glad to see them.

When David and Caitlin visit, pet care and animals in general are two of the few available topics for discussion. I'm not afraid to bring up religion or politics, but even before the pageant, we found room to disagree. We all profess to be Democrats, but David is more like what you'd call a swing voter, Caitlin is more like what you'd call a non-voter, and Meredith and I once tried volunteering with the Payne County Democrats, but gave up after the regional chairperson kept asking us to coach her daughter's basketball team in exchange for the loan of her grandmother's wedding dress, a family heirloom, she said, something to legitimize our union. David has always had dogs—though he leaves his at home—and Caitlin has a horse she shows down in Florida. So when we run out of things to talk about—as we often do—we always return to animal care: curry combs, choke chains, farriers and flea powder, you name, it, we've talked about it, usually at some length. Sometimes, after a long bout of silence after which we've exhausted all the usual conversations about the weather, diets, and new construction around town, Meredith will dig out one of her pet care catalogs and read aloud from the ad copy. Caitlin grabs her purse, fishes for her credit card and phone, and orders a new water bowl, chew toy, or tiny T-shirt for Mayonnaise. David acts all broke and beleaguered and returns to the television, and Meredith and I play keep away with our own dogs while Mayonnaise barks away on the sidelines.

One thing to know about Mayonnaise is that he hates David. He particularly hates a certain turn of phrase David uses fairly often—"recipe for disaster." Every time David says something like, "Oh wow, Caitlin on the Cimarron Turnpike, 80 miles an hour, a recipe for disaster," the dog sounds the alarm and the neighbors across the street call their small children inside where it's safe. For this reason, both Meredith and I like Mayonnaise a great deal. Our aging pit bulls, too, have a special affection for Mayonnaise and the youthful canine energy he brings with him. We value Mayonnaise's presence not only for its comic effect, but also for its bravery. I, too, dislike David's use of the phrase, "recipe for disaster." Who doesn't? But who among us has the guts to say so? Mayonnaise, that's who. Our pal.

After the deadly trio of David, Caitlin, and Mayonnaise stepped onto the porch, Meredith led them inside to the room she calls the sewing room and I call "the extra room," since I can't recall the last time anyone did any sewing in that room or, really, anywhere in the entire house. We all agreed Caitlin and Mayonnaise would take the non-sewing room and David would take the couch in the living room. This meant he would stay up all night watching, as he did the last time he visited, boxing matches from the 1970s and news reports from Japan. We have one of those premium cable packages meant for people who live out in the country—a thousand channels from around the world, all promising to provide compensation for the emptiness and isolation that has become your daily life. Meredith and I hardly ever watch, but David, like most men, seems to take comfort from the dancing colors on the screen. After we helped them unload their remaining belongings from the car, Meredith gave David a beer and we waved him off until dinner time.

So far, no one had mentioned the pageant, though Caitlin's gaze, as the day wore on, took on a strange, almost sickly quality, as if she had swallowed a key or, more likely, started on an adjusted dosage of antidepressants. Her skin, normally a beautiful bronze produced by the magic of spray-on tanning products, appeared pale and drawn, her hair brittle and thin, her lips like lost amphibians. And she's normally very chatty—full of talk about recent outings with her friends, term papers she's had to write, the usual college fare—but the pageant seemed to have silenced her, taken away what she might have called her own optimism, David might have called her innocence, and Meredith I might have called her foolishness. She seemed more careful now, and more forbidding. When I asked her if she preferred Diet Coke or water, she looked past me out the window and said, "I prefer Niagara Falls. Mother always said the falls were in Canada, but she lied." So you see the kind of thing I'm talking about. I tried not to laugh and gave her a glass of water, the bottled kind, something supposedly from a natural spring somewhere, but in actuality from the Las Vegas municipal supply.

"I'm sorry," Caitlin said. She hadn't touched the bottle of water. *You sure are.* Of all the insincere remarks so prevalent among American youth, "I'm sorry" is perhaps the least likely to pack a punch in terms of true sentiment. You're talking to a *librarian* here, I wanted to say. No matter if you loaned the book to your boyfriend and he left it in the trunk of his Chevy Nova. No matter if you *meant* to log off the computer. No matter if you washed your library card in the back pocket of your McDonald's uniform. No matter if you forgot to push your chair underneath the table, or use your inside voice, or replace the current copy of *Field & Stream* in its proper place between *Family Circle* and *Forbes*. The damage is already done.

"No need to be sorry," I said. "You can have Diet

Coke with dinner if you like."

Meredith, after filling a plastic cup with ice and offering Caitlin a bendable straw, brought cheese and crackers to the table. "The pageant," she said. "Let's talk."

"No talking," David said from the living room. "Not until the game is over."

"We'll talk later," I said. "For now, let's just admire this cheese here. Meredith, where did you buy this cheese?"

"I hate cheese," Caitlin said.

"Bring it in here," David said.

I've always suspected David preferred Meredith to me. And when Caitlin was twelve, she made a three-dimensional family-tree project at summer camp that included Meredith—and our dogs!—and left me out entirely. Meredith has an easy way about her; she's the kind of person others like to take into their confidence. I, on the other hand, tend to inspire rage and confusion. Or, at least, I wish I did. Really, I inspire boredom. The truth is Caitlin left me off the family-tree project because she forgot about me, since her visits to our house had become more and more infrequent after her family moved to Florida. Why she remembered Meredith and the dogs I don't know.

Later, Meredith joined David in front of the television, and I asked Caitlin to join me at the barn. It was too wet to ride, but I wanted to show off the boarding facility's newest addition, a magnificent chestnut Hanoverian schoolmaster that a much wealthier friend was allowing me to ride while she taught for a semester overseas. In the car, on the way to the barn, I made a decision. I would pretend the horse belonged to me.

A storm had passed through the night before, and the sky, large like a worn set of curtains, seemed to curl around us at the edges. A gust of wind swept brown leaves against the walls of the barn. Most of the horses had been turned out, but an injured "world champion" Appaloosa gelding wearing a cribbing collar remained, downtrodden and disheveled, in a stall by the door. Caitlin took a special interest in the injured horse; I think he reminded her of her father, or, at least, the sick and the lame always reminded *me* of her father. Wisely, we had decided to leave Mayonnaise at home. But Caitlin missed him. Pageants and pageant rehearsals aside, he accompanied her everywhere.

"I could have carried him," she said. "He would have loved it here."

I told another lie: the property-owner didn't allow outside animals. In part, this was true. The barn's list of rules included the plea to "please leave dogs at home," but this rule, like so many others, was only half-heartedly enforced. Really, I didn't want Mayonnaise there because his bark would have annoyed the horses, and plus, he would have proven a distraction from my crowning glory—Arge the Barge, the magnificent seventeen-hand, well-mannered Hanoverian unfortunately belonging to someone else. I guess Caitlin suspected as much.

"You have the papers?" she said. "Is he registered?"

"He's double-registered," another lie, though double-registry, in this case, would have been neither necessary nor impressive. But Caitlin wouldn't know. She would know only what I chose to tell her. Arge the Barge stood near the door to his paddock; he was a sweet old thing,

full of friendly ambition. Inside his paddock were a water trough and hay rack, but the ground was barren and
dry—not a blade of grass for many miles around. As
always, I carried dried apple treats and a carrot in the
front pocket of my jacket. Arge nosed his way through
the rails of the fence and nibbled with affection at the
tail of my shirt. I loved Arge, and I thought Caitlin
failed to adequately appreciate his beauty. I suggested
we groom him.

"I don't want to get dirty," Caitlin said.

"Sure you do."

She finally agreed, after which we made our way
to the tack room across the gravel lane. Though ten
or fifteen other locals boarded there, the place was de-
serted—the horses and a couple of mean barn cats were
our only company. I unlocked the tack room, a dusty
corner of the barn about the size of a walk-in closet,
and Caitlin followed me in.

What I thought was another gust of wind slammed
the door shut behind us. Had Caitlin closed the door?
The tack room was really very small. There we were, the
two of us, wedged between an ancient Western saddle
and a twenty-pound bag of alfalfa cubes, a bottle of fly
spray leaking a slow drip from a shelf in the corner. She
had me trapped there. Normally, Caitlin is the kind of
person who blinks rapidly when she speaks directly to
another person—a defense mechanism, a fearful mixture of vanity and insecurity. But in the small space and
dim light of the tack room, I could see her eyes wide
open in the manner of exaggerated victims in horror
films meant for teenagers.

"Why don't you and Meredith ever get married?"

"Hand me that plastic bag," I said. "I bought some new brushes."

"Really," she said. "You can't go on like this forever."

"Like what?"

"Living in sin."

I couldn't help myself: I laughed. Looking back, I suppose I should not have allowed her misplaced moralism to bother me as much as it did. I tried to remind myself she was only a child; she didn't know any better. If gay marriage happened to be all the rage these days, Caitlin, like a dog on the scent of squirrel, would follow the tolerance trend with rapid obedience. I knew she hadn't meant what she said in her pageant interview—not really, anyway—and I knew she probably would sing a different tune tomorrow. For a moment, I considered the various causes and callings of her pageant competitors: calisthenics for cancer victims, computers for coffee farmers, backpacks for children without books. Maybe marriage *should be* between a man and a woman. If Caitlin thought Meredith and I were living in sin, maybe we were doing something right.

I took what I thought was a judicious approach and asked Caitlin why she was suddenly so concerned about sin. I asked her, too, when she had started going to church.

"It's called Life Church," she said. By now, she had opened the door to the tack room and allowed my escape into the aisle of the barn. "It's very accepting of alternative lifestyles."

I pretended I was too busy, too uninterested to

reply. I walked past her through the barn's open door. Outside, it was starting to rain. I pulled Arge the Barge out of his paddock and tied him to the front of his stall. A few feet away, the lame Appaloosa kicked at the wall of the barn, a steady rhythm of boredom and despair. Caitlin stood near the door to his stall and tried to calm him with the slow sound of her voice. For a while, I combed Arge's tail and said nothing. I had to admit Caitlin had a way with horses. She was able to convince the Appaloosa to stop kicking the wall, and, as a result, a welcome silence settled onto the barn. With quiet deliberation, she brought a brush from the tack room and approached "my" horse with considerable care. She scratched Arge behind his withers; she liked him, I could tell, but she didn't want to *own* him, as I had intended. In fact, she said several times he "seemed to be holding up rather well," an unmistakable coded phrase for old and broken down.

I asked Caitlin about her father. Since my first encounter with David, he had always been a bit of a show-off, the kind of person who played multiple musical instruments, danced in public, and told mean jokes about money-grubbing TV evangelists and politicians caught with their pants down. For all his faults, he didn't seem like the Life Church type.

"It's *his* church," she said. "You know my photographer?" Here she launched into a not-so-catchy jingle for what must have been a staple of her local television networks: *That's William Hamburger of Hamburger Photography, Wellington, West Palm: Digital Proofs and a Whole Lotta Beef.*"

I said, "I remember."

"They go together," she said. She looked at the ground and continued, her voice grave and low. "Dad and William go to Life Church. Together."

I'll admit I was surprised. Flabbergasted is more like it. All right, so David had exhausted his womanizing phase. One could travel only so far down the path of hot-rodding middle-aged male-pattern baldness. One could pick up only so many women before women started to seem easy, distracting, boring. I realized Meredith and I had become unwitting pawns in a great game of gay acceptance. Caitlin, too, had been duped. What she thought was a winning strategy at the pageant had backfired and blossomed into a full-blown media circus as well as a source of shame for her newly-gay father, David, the wild widower. Worse, they all had become religious fanatics. Gay religious fanatics. Just what the world needed.

"So you all go to Life Church," I said. "Together?"

"I don't sit with them," she said. "He wants me to."

"Your dad?"

"Not my dad," she said. "William."

"And your dad?"

"He doesn't care."

I returned to combing out Arge's mane and tail. Together, Caitlin and I removed all but the finest particles of red dirt from his coat. We were nearly finished when Caitlin said, "I really am sorry. About the pageant. I wanted to piss off my dad. You know."

"Did it work?" I said.

"He was pretty mad," she said. "But he never

mentioned William. All he would say was that I had hurt Meredith's feelings. And yours."

It was not lost on me that she had mentioned Meredith first. And David, before her, had mentioned Meredith first. Long ago, David married my sister, not Meredith's. But my sister was dead, of course, and it seemed to me everyone was taking full advantage of her absence.

I should have known William Hamburger would be at our house when we got home. He had followed behind them in his Ford Escort all the way from Florida. *Of course* someone named William Hamburger would drive a Ford Escort. What else could I expect? On the drive home, before Caitlin spotted the Escort in our driveway, I thought about old Bill Burger and his greasy pony-tail, his diamond stud earring, his tattoo of a bleeding heart right there on his neck, where everyone could see. I had met him once before, years ago at a New Year's Eve party in Boca Raton. Meredith and I were celebrating our anniversary, a vacation of sorts, an excuse to take a trip and see relatives at the same time. My sister was still alive. Now, in my own backyard, watching as Meredith laughed (politely, I assumed) at one of William Hamburger's jokes, it occurred to me this man was something like Caitlin's stepfather, and I wondered at first how she must have felt about him. She, too, seemed to expect he would be there, or at least, she betrayed nothing in terms of surprise when we saw the Escort in the driveway.

I should mention we keep giant tortoises in our backyard. Looking out the window, I could see Meredith and

Bill Burger sitting together on a wrap-around bench underneath our river birch tree. They appeared as if deep in conversation, Meredith's hand cupped around her chin, Bill Burger's gestures growing more and more exaggerated. David, holding out a crust of bread, crouched to meet the gaze of a tortoise, the senior male, the one with an incurable fungus on its feet. I envied their considerable ease. I knew, too, the fun would come to an immediate end if I opened the back door and joined them in the yard. Caitlin must have been thinking the same thing because she made a move for the door and stopped herself, her hand in midair between the safety of her front pocket and the danger of the doorknob. I watched as she sat at the kitchen table and turned her head toward the window.

To make the most of having houseguests, one must first pretend to be gracious. I remembered this rule as I arranged cookies on a platter and assembled a centerpiece from a bud vase—without a bud—and the porcelain pit bull figurines David presented to us upon his arrival. I watched as Caitlin, like Dustin Hoffman in *The Graduate*, pressed her palms against the kitchen window's glass. The trip to the barn at first seemed to diminish her overall strangeness, but now it was back with a vengeance.

"No more cheese," she said, as if in a trance. "I'll die if you serve cheese."

I told her the cookies I was serving contained a long list of healthy ingredients, even offered to peel some carrots to go with them, but she seemed not to hear me. Outside, the merriment continued. We could hear laughter erupting in occasional loud bursts, and Caitlin cringed every time David's voice rose above the others. When I heard Meredith say something like, *who knew you could have so much fun with Popsicle sticks,* I decided I would not prepare dinner and order a pizza instead.

When they came back inside, they were still laughing, but they did not have William Hamburger with them.

"Where's your, uh, friend?" I said.

"Photo shoot in Dallas," David said. "He had to run."

"He couldn't even come inside to say hello?"

David and Meredith laughed, a cruel knowing laugh, as if they had talked about what I would say when I heard the news. Caitlin looked up from the window and said, "Our lives are ruled by chance meetings."

Everyone ignored her and began to eat the cookies, though I'll admit they didn't taste very good. Meredith, always one to plan activities, had the idea we should give the dogs a bath before dinner. David seemed pleased, excited even, as he went for towels in the linen closet in the hallway. Caitlin insisted Mayonnaise didn't need a bath, but Meredith brought out some botanical collection canine shampoo, opened the pop-top, and held the bottle under Caitlin's nose until she seemed impressed with the honeysuckle scent and called Mayonnaise in from the guest room where he had been napping in a laundry basket in the closet.

David pushed Caitlin out of the way so he could smell the shampoo.

"Use baby shampoo," he said. "Some people say baby shampoo is for babies, but I know better. Baby shampoo is for babies, dogs, regular-sized people, cars, scrubbing the kitchen floor, and washing dishes when you run out of dish soap. Really, it's good for everything."

"Dad," Caitlin said. "They don't have any baby shampoo."

Here is where Meredith started to annoy me. She's what the pop-psychologists would call a people-pleaser. "I can run out and buy some," she said. "Johnson & Johnson, right? Or have they changed the name?"

"We don't need baby shampoo," I said.

"I'll just run to the store."

Caitlin said, "Don't bother."

"No bother."

"I'm bothered," I said. "Shampoo decisions should be between an owner and her dog."

An awkward silence returned to the room. Maybe they didn't understand my joke. Maybe they understood all too well. David searched the fridge for another beer, Caitlin stared out the window at the rusty barbecue grill on our back deck, Meredith pretended to load the dishwasher, and I looked up at a framed lithograph above our fireplace: two Amazon parrots overlooking the ocean. Welcome to paradise.

Mayonnaise, his coat kept a creamy white by virtue of his feet rarely touching the ground, loves baths almost as much as he loves playing with our two pit bulls. Our pit bulls, however, hate baths and always have. Knowing this, I suggested we give each dog an individual bath rather than try for some big group activity of family fun.

"We have them outnumbered," David said. "Four humans. Three dogs. They don't stand a chance."

"Come on, Aunties," Caitlin said, her gaze returning

to the table. "It'll be fun."

Then, Meredith: the ultimate betrayal. Maybe she was still mad about the thing with the baby shampoo. "You're too rigid, Sally."

Our bathroom is really quite small. And it was too cold outside to use the garden hose. And David is rather portly. And Caitlin insisted on wearing her bathing suit and sending multiple text messages or tweets or whatever they are to announce the upcoming bath and the bath-in-progress and the post-bath search for extra beach towels in the linen closet in the hall. And our pit bulls are much too heavy to lift into the bathtub. You see where this is going. It didn't go well.

I had hurt my back lifting the pit bulls, but all the dogs were behaving better than expected. My pants rolled at the ankles, I stepped one leg into the tub in an emergency attempt to keep Mayonnaise from drinking the soapy water. Meredith and Caitlin both said they didn't want to get wet—they just wanted to watch, they said, and help out if one of the dogs tried to make a break for it—so David and I engaged in a kind of blind man's dance, our arms and legs at various times intertwined, knees and elbows locked, hands grabbing at fistfuls of fur. I felt a fool repeating futile commands to the dogs while David remained mostly silent except to complain about the humidity in the bathroom. His skin, he said, would suffer as a result. The dog shampoo, too, was giving him a rash.

"A recipe for disaster," he said, and that's when I felt a flash of the future: I would take Caitlin out of my will, Meredith would take a programming job out of state, David would marry William Hamburger in the state of Massachusetts, Arge the Barge would return to his rightful owner, Caitlin would drop out of college and become a "dancer" and also a spokesperson for the religious right, my pit bulls would die, my giant tortoise would succumb to the fungus on his feet, and I, anonymously ashamed of being neither married nor divorced, would be truly single for the first time in twenty years, alone in this empty house in empty Oklahoma.

Right on schedule, Mayonnaise took a chunk of David's leg in between his tight little teeth. "Oh my god," he said. "Get the little bastard off of me."

Meredith started laughing, a mistake, I knew, but I didn't stop her. I grabbed at the place where Mayonnaise's collar would be, but he had latched on to the fatty part of David's calf and was not about to let go for my sake.

Caitlin dropped her phone and leapt into action. Get away from my dog, she said. Goddamn you. Goddamn fags.

Mayonnaise didn't break the skin, but later, after the shocked silence and the realization I would be the one to scrub out the bathtub, David came into the bathroom to wrap his leg with gauze. He had the toilet seat down and his leg propped up for inspection.

It didn't really hurt, he said, and I said sure, he's just a little dog, next time we'll see what the pit bulls can do. And though I didn't really mean to hurt anyone, I closed the shower curtain on the clean bathtub and said something like don't be such a baby, David, you'll have to stand up for yourself for once and have that dog put down.

Three Stories of Prosperity

1

At the end of a long day overseeing the overseas manu-
facture of drinking straws, a rich man, in the midst of
removing his shoes, sees a mouse. *Eek*, he says, ironic
because he never before has said the word "eek," never
before thought himself fearful of skittering or stinging
creatures; mostly he looks only at papers and a computer
screen, car keys and, not very often, piano keys when
he feels like indulging his artistic side. But today he
sees a mouse. Today he says—but does not shout—the
word "eek," only no one is home to hear him.

Eek, he says again, because he can. *A mouse.*

The mouse, brown and lumpy like an old crust of
bread, hobbles along in fits and starts by the fireplace.
The fireplace is empty save a single desiccated log and
a pile of ashes, cold below the drafts in the chimney.
The rich man realizes at once the mouse is ill, poisoned
perhaps, taken over by tumors, nervous and useless
and heaving from the depths of its twisted innards.
The mouse sputters and gags, staggers and limps, and
finally cowers in a corner, its uneven breathing like

loose grit blown against windowpanes during a storm. The rich man decides against removing his shoes and instead reties their laces, puts on tomorrow's necktie, and prepares himself against the winter wind outside. He buttons his overcoat, finds an old fuzzy hat he wore when he was a boy and ties it underneath his chin. A pair of gloves meant for below-zero temperatures make him look like an astronaut, the whole world a vacuum, gravity be damned. He has some idea he'll find a shovel in the garage, scoop up the mouse, and dump it outside in the elements until nature takes its course.

He abandons this idea as too sensible and instead takes a water glass from the kitchen cabinet, overturns it, and places it, dome-like, on top of the mouse, now, thanks to his handiwork, a specimen enclosed for observation, an artifact bound for a museum, like the bullet that killed Abraham Lincoln or the left hemisphere of Einstein's brain.

He looks closer at the mouse-under-glass, its laboring lungs and convulsing limbs. All at once he is speaking to the mouse, even though he has never before spoken to a mouse, never had cause to speak to a mouse, never even thought about mice very much at all unless you counted the time he set traps for an old neighbor when he was a boy.

Something's going to happen to me tomorrow, he says. *Something terrible is going to happen to me. I'm going to eat my breakfast and drive my car and walk into my building and greet my secretary and stamp my seal of approval and come home just like I always do, only something terrible is going to happen, tomorrow, when I least expect it. Oh little mouse, I could drink you like I'd drink a glass of water.*

2

On the first Saturday in November, the University Alumni Association sponsors the Spurs 'n' Saddle Black Tie Barbecue, tuxedos and cowboy boots only, please; ladies, evening gowns and stockings, leave your roping pants at home. Eileen believes herself so rich she can wear anything she wants, but she is mistaken, as she discovers, when she shows up twenty minutes early wearing jeans and a diamond-studded sweater, her hair braided with ribbons honoring the school colors, also the colors of Halloween. She believes the event a potluck, another mistake, as she realizes when the wife of the university president takes one look at her casserole dish and says, *You must be allergic.* As if she would bring her own food to compensate for her shellfish allergy, and so what if she's given up red meat, who do these people think they are, anyway? Eileen herself comes from new money, but then so does everyone else in this backwater town. All the old money travels in a rusted-out pipeline down to the Gulf of Mexico. Eileen's husband—often mistaken for her father—is a periodontist and a part-time airline pilot, moonlighting for the sake of their big house on the outskirts of town. And their children have not distinguished themselves as children around here should. The oldest—a girl—wants to become an opera singer and the younger one—a boy—has disappointed everyone first by refusing football, then by giving up golf lessons, and finally, against the explicit wishes of his father, joining the symphony orchestra as the first-chair flautist, a prodigy at the tender age of twelve. What is to be done about such artistic children? Eileen envies friends from the Alumni Association whose children are autistic and not artistic, at least those weirdos could be cured with a pill. But she does her best to encourage her own children; she's proud of them, in her way, and their gifts, such as they are, might reap financial rewards or, at the very least, help her daughter find a husband and her son find a wife. Really she's not that cold. Really she's very warm. Really she wants what's best for them, what's best for the family, a mention in the local paper, a smile and a nod from the Republican state senator. Really she didn't mean to bring a casserole to the Spurs 'n' Saddle Black Tie Barbecue, a catered event, and really she didn't mean to wear jeans.

Better to be comfortable, says the wife of the university president. *And to think it might rain.* The wife of the university president is also named Eileen. Privately, Eileen thinks of herself as Eileen #1 and the wife of the university president as Eileen #2, a reversal of sorts, but one that does not fail to please.

Eileen #2's pronouncement turns out to be prophetic: the Spurs 'n' Saddle Black Tie Barbecue suffers under a deluge, the sky flattens and opens with a sudden sideways slant, as if the rainwater were the trick of a magician's assistant, the mass of clouds a secret trapdoor. Both Eileens escape under an awning, the entrance to the Hotel and Restaurant School's flagship teaching establishment, a fancy steakhouse with cloth napkins and a fireplace, The Ranchers Club, they call it, though no ranchers ever dine there. In a glass case on the wall is the menu, items listed in calligraphy, barbed wire bordering the edges, steaks and more steaks, potatoes, the vegetable of the day. Next to the menu is the painted profile of a cow, its round body and lean flanks meant to suggest the decadence of the savory experience to come. Eileen #1 steps back from the awning's edge when the rainwater shoots toward her in a horizontal splash; now she's next to the menu, eye to eye with the outline of the cow. She's not sure, but for a moment she thinks she catches the cow looking at her diamond-studded sweater and the ribbons in her hair. No, it's really happening, the cow is staring her down, its eyeball a bulging yellow mass, and the rain's coming harder now, great gusts of pressurized spray, like water from the hoses they use to clean the killing-room floor.

3

Brandon is a banker, or at least well on his way. For now, he's the loan officer at a local branch of Appletree Savings and Loan, "a deposit a day keeps the landlord away." He's like Jimmy Stewart in *It's a Wonderful Life*, only not as stupid, he thinks, not as prone to sentimental mistakes. He's recently divorced, lying alone in bed one night when the telephone rings, something that never happens anymore, not even during the day. He rolls over, shakes off a vague dream of sunlight on the floor of a barn, and answers.

Hello, he says. *Mom?*

She knows some people, she says, some people who need a loan.

Right now? he says. *They need a loan in the middle of the night?*

Please, she says. *They're lesbians.*

Brandon is open-minded, and he watches a lot of television. His former brother-in-law, his high-school history teacher, two and a possible third teller at Appletree Saving and Loan: all gay. All fine with him. And if they had the right credit scores, sure, he'd give them a loan, no problemo, amigo, amigas, mujeres con mujeres, whatever floats your boat. The time, though, is troubling. *Tomorrow,* he says to his mother. *Have them call me at the bank tomorrow.*

Okay, his mother says before hanging up. *Okay?*

Well, okay, then. It's all settled. Tomorrow he will work. *Something terrible is going to happen to him, tomorrow. He's going to eat his breakfast and drive his car and walk into his building and stamp his seal of approval and come home just like he always does, only something terrible is going to happen, tomorrow, when he least expects it.* He doesn't have a secretary, but maybe if he did, all this trouble would go away. He's tired now, his body like a limpid stream, floating, drifting off to sleep. He returns to the dream of sunlight on the floorboards of his grandfather's big, red barn, only the paint is fading and flaking, the boards loose and rotting, the whole thing turning pink before his very eyes. *Who will pay the mortgage every month? Who will cook the dinner? Who will change the furnace filter? If they find a wasp nest in the eaves, who will knock it down? Who will fold the laundry? Who will mow the lawn?*

Glue

The sun, bright and blinding like an accounting-inspired headache, shone through the rear window of the bus one day when Polly sneezed and lost a tooth. She was neither young enough for baby teeth nor old enough for dentures, so the loss of the tooth was a mystery. She never ate pistachios, never removed bottle caps with anything but an opener, never, to her knowledge, stiffened her jaw during sleep. In fact, she wished she were the kind of person for whom dental hygiene was an afterthought. She imagined herself a freewheeling party girl, someone who might, in the manner of a recent popular song, "drill the dentist with the hard stuff." But she was scrupulous about brushing and flossing both, and friends always said she ought to star in commercials for tooth-whitening strips. The bus had just pulled away from the curb—Polly, seated, as always in the third row—when the tooth, bloodless and painless, came out in her hand.

She shared her seat with another passenger, a regular rider who happened to be retarded, or near-retarded, or maybe you weren't supposed to say retarded these days, but this man was undeniably different, slow, but not childlike, chatty, but not sweet.

"She lost a tooth," the slow man announced to the other passengers—two students sharing the same backpack, an old man, also retarded, shouting into a cell phone, a woman wiping the nose of a sick child. The slow man's announcement blended in with the rest of the morning's noise, and the passengers went on with their business. The slow man took their indifference to suggest he ought to speak louder.

"Hey, everybody," he said. "This girl's a jack-o-lantern."

Polly rode the bus to work every day, and every day was the same, or something like it, the same rush for keys and coffee, the same pleading look from the dog—*don't go, don't go*—the same walk through the same wet grass in the front yard, her shoes once again soaked through, the same conversation with herself about whether she had time enough to step inside to replace her wet socks with dry ones. No time, she never had time, so she continued by stepping lightly, avoiding puddles and sticking to the patches of weedy gravel on the way to the bus stop. What was she afraid of? She was afraid of what people thought of her—foolish, really, since mostly they didn't think much at all. Their complacency only compounded her loneliness, her secret wish for notoriety. She was reliable, yes, but she planned for an imagined future in which she was dangerous, volatile, free. Others would think of her always, planning revenge plots or hoping to ruin her reputation on the Internet. As it stood now, most people seemed to find her merely entertaining, or, if they thought of her in more generous terms, their thoughts came with the knowledge she would always be there, like the dew on the morning grass, like a pair of scissors kept in the junk drawer underneath the telephone, like a lucky piece of twine, like glue.

Her job, among other, mostly useless, duties was to keep the law office stocked with large numbers of office supplies no one would ever use—account ledgers long ago replaced by Excel spreadsheets, legal pads used mainly to keep children busy when their parents dragged them along to the office, typewriter ribbons from 1974. She considered obsolete office supplies a kind of specialty; she was a collector, a historian of the mimeograph machine and the ten-pound tape dispenser. She kept these items in full view, on a long line of shelves covering the back wall of the law office. And because no one paid attention to the office supply budget or the UPS man's frequent deliveries, she ordered whatever she liked: film projectors and dictation machines, broken staple guns off eBay, reams of colored paper printed with still-familiar slogans from Bill Clinton's campaign for re-election. The upper brass considered it a hobby of hers, a negligible idiosyncrasy, something to distinguish *their* paralegal from the boring, faceless business majors haunting the halls of all the other local law firms, their competitors, though this was Market Town: not much action.

Polly had neither boyfriend nor husband nor secret crush among the regular passengers on the bus. What she did have was a long-standing imaginary relationship with a woman, an older woman, an older *married* woman, an older married woman who once was her boss at the law firm, a beautiful woman named Margaret Kendall of Kendall, Lember, and Long. Margaret Kendall was one of Market Town's most upstanding citizens—she even ran for mayor once and lost. But Margaret departed months ago, leaving Polly and the law firm behind so as to follow her husband, also one of Market Town's most upstanding citizens, a history professor at the university, to his new job as something like guy-in-charge-of-Abraham-Lincoln-stuff in the Obama administration. Polly missed Margaret terribly. At work, Margaret had been both magnanimous and demanding, the kind of boss who remembered people's birthdays and mopped up her own spills in the microwave, but also liked it when lawyers stayed late and was not afraid to shame people for sloppiness. She once told a judge in court, *hey, wake up there, big guy,* and another time she told a Mormon missionary to try his luck in the pits of hell. Margaret liked Polly, too, or at least she seemed to. She brought Polly along to all the important depositions and included her in clandestine meetings even the senior partners were not allowed to attend. And they were friends, too, in a long lunch and occasional cocktail hour kind of way. Early on, Polly developed a habit of writing Margaret a daily e-mail she lacked the courage to send, always ending with the fateful words, *we ought to have dinner sometime.* No big deal, really, a request for dinner, but Polly lived in constant fear her secret attraction would come to light, her reputation ruined, her humiliation all but guaranteed when Margaret sent her gently on her way. Now that Margaret had moved away, Polly took a twisted kind of solace from her fair share of romantic regrets and the lasting memory of Margaret's sure presence on the other side of the conference room door. But Margaret was gone, and Polly forced herself to move on. Determined herself to leave Market Town one day, she'd applied to several law schools out of state and checked her mailbox two and sometimes three times a day for the results. She couldn't break the e-mail habit, though; she wrote to Margaret, or some imagined version of Margaret, every night after her second glass of wine.

Always she told Margaret about her morning ride on the bus. *Dear Margaret.* (Or sometimes the more jaunty *Hi, Margaret!*) *Rode the bus again today. I lost a tooth. No one noticed, except for Slow Bo.* Slow Bo lived in a group home mysteriously called The Sheltered Workshop two blocks from Polly's one-bedroom "starter home," itself a former headquarters for those responsible for the sheltering at the Sheltered Workshop, a house turned office turned house once again.

Once, after waking to a strange noise in the middle of the night, Polly discovered something called a behavioral checklist inside the workbench built into the garage. She had been looking for a flashlight, or maybe some kind of tool she could use as a weapon, when she found instead the handwritten evaluation list pasted inside a rotting file folder: *feeds himself, cleans himself, can perform basic tasks such as grating cheese.* Every time she rode the bus with Slow Bo, she wondered how he had fared on the behavioral checklist—could he, for example, be relied upon to dress in seasonally-appropriate attire? Did he remain within budget during weekly trips to Walmart? Did he ruin dinner by throwing what the behavioral checklist called "taco meat" against the wall of the kitchen? She searched her kitchen for stains, but concluded they must have painted the place before turning it over to the realtor and moving into their new and improved—more sheltered—headquarters, a sleek, modern facility named after a wealthy benefactor, none other than Margaret's upstanding history-professing husband, expert on Abraham Lincoln, a cold and methodical man, a product of old Market Town money, himself rumored to be gay. Now that he worked for the Obama administration he was not gay at all—the right-wing radio commentators would have a field day with that one—but Polly suspected theirs was a marriage of convenience, nonetheless. For this reason, she held out a faint hope Margaret would return to Market Town alone, maybe heartbroken and maybe relieved, either way she'd be single, either way she'd be free. Foolish, she thought, to create a future from thin air.

Every night she wrote Margaret an imaginary e-mail full of confessions, anecdotes, dreams, and failures. And all of her meanderings seemed harmless enough until—and this was unexpected—Margaret wrote back.

Polly, she said. *You're cruel. Consider the loss of your tooth a symptom and not a disease. Your passivity is not just an inconvenience but a malady. Your thoughts are like blankets in summertime, like a basement without windows, like a pantry full of ten-pound bags of flour, like glue.*

The screen of Polly's laptop glowed with a pulsating energy, every pixel a starburst, every word a reentry into the realm of the impossible. Since Polly had never actually sent any of her daily e-mails to Margaret, the message now appearing on the screen seemed at first like something she must have written herself and then later forgotten. She considered the possibility she was going crazy. Did the experts have a term these days for textual hallucination? Surely some poor girl somewhere had imagined herself receiving text messages from some Twittering teen heartthrob. She checked all the e-mail's authenticating watermarks—the "To" and "From" fields, the brand name of the provider, the signature and the date. Everything seemed in order; in fact, the phantom Margaret had used her secret e-mail address, the one only friends and relatives knew, the one Polly had congratulated herself for memorizing after a close encounter in the Xerox room one day, a first in her long series of snooping expeditions in which she spotted all of Margaret's seven e-mail addresses printed on some kind of grant application.

On the bus, she thought of Margaret and Geoffrey cutting a fine figure in Dupont Circle and Georgetown, their fingers curved around stemware, their heads thrown back in laughter. Like Polly, Slow Bo rode the bus alone. Because of his daily, unsupervised appearance at the bus stop, she decided he must have scored better on the behavioral checklist than some of the others, the shuffling, messy-haired mob she sometimes saw around town attached to a single leash, their wrists secured to a plastic lanyard with clips and lines that resembled mountain-climbing equipment, only this was Oklahoma, not a mountain in sight. On Mondays, Wednesdays, and Friday, Polly and Slow Bo were the only passengers on the bus, and the driver, that grunt-ing, faceless fat man with a buzz cut, might have been the same, might have been different—they rotated the drivers every week or so—but all of them wore the same gruff exterior, the company uniform for the corporate entity called "Big Orange Bus" or, for the townies, BOB.

Slow Bo liked to talk, and because his chosen sub-jects were usually some variation on "bus" and "break-fast," Polly usually brought along a library book or her iPod. One day on the way to the bus stop, a pickup truck almost hit her in the middle of "Swingtime Saturday,"—she hadn't heard its roaring engine over the sound of the trombone section—so, fearing for her safety, she had taken to leaving the iPod at home. Also, she had stopped reading books ever since Margaret left town, her comprehension limited to short and very frequent forays into the world of online "news." Because this means of avoidance had lately failed her, Polly had no choice but to nod—and try to smile—when Slow Bo began to speak.

"You like Obama?" he said. Slow Bo was short, maybe 5'3", in his mid-forties, with a receding hairline and big, boxy eyeglasses like Clark Kent's, only Bo's frames were orange—"like the bus!" he said—and they were so heavy and awkward they slipped down the bridge of his nose, a problem he solved by slamming his face against the soft side of Polly's seat. He had a characteristic way of repeating himself: three nods instead of one, four extra foot-stomps after stepping onto the bus, five or six rapid tugs at his earlobe when a siren passed by. Sometimes he slapped his thigh so hard he must have left bruises when he patted his pockets for change. His speech patterns mimicked his gestures so that he often said things like "yes, yes, yes," and "on the bus, there's the bus, where's the bus?"

Polly nodded. "Yes. There's another bus."

"You like Obama?" he said again. "'Cause I like Obama. I voted for Obama. You?"

"Yes," Polly said. "You had to."

"You had to?" Slow Bo said. "Somebody made you?"

"Sort of," she said.

"Somebody made you vote for Obama," he said, as the bus approached the Student Union Food Court where he worked. He clomped up to the driver, slapped his thigh, pointed at Polly, and said, "Somebody made her vote for Obama."

The driver grunted in response, doubtless an expression of disapproval or even simmering rage. Polly had learned to conceal her politics in public, though the lawyers in the firm were mostly Democrats, the Oklahoma kind, gutless and religious in an obligatory way, their weekends full of the meaningless chatter of backyard barbecues, volunteer work on the boards of benevolent organizations, boating on the lake, bragging about the kids. But the lawyers were the best she could hope for, really, since the general population was made up of people like the bus driver, resentful right-wingers and quasi-libertarians; you might call them Tea Partiers if they had more energy, but their lethargy made them seem more like tea sippers or teapot polishers, boring old bigots.

"I like Obama," Bo said every day since the election.

And when his namesake joined the first family in the form of a Portuguese waterdog, Slow Bo was ecstatic. "Bo Bama," he said at least a thousand times a day. "You like Bo Bama?"

"Sure," Polly said. "He's cute."

"'Cause I like Bo Bama."

"Yeah."

"You like Bo Bama?"

"Yeah," she said again. They passed a row of silver maples by the side of the road, twenty or more, each one just like all the others.

"Hey, everybody," Bo said, even though they were once again the only passengers on the bus. "Me and her like Bo Bama."

This was the usual way of things for a while—sometimes Polly brought her iPod and sometimes she left it at home—until the news broke that the First Dog had bitten—nibbled, really—a couple of schoolchildren visiting the White House. It was spring, just after Easter, and Polly tried to imagine the cherry blossoms beginning to bloom on Pennsylvania Avenue. There was Margaret, her eyes on a pair of pigeons, her fingers stretched behind her to reach for the belt hanging loose around her long, wool coat. Had she been invited to the White House that day? Slow Bo wouldn't know. Slow Bo didn't even realize something had gone wrong at the First Lady's question-and-answer session, hadn't read the news reports of Secret Service agents ushering the dog out of the crowded room and back to the safety of the East Wing. Instead, he was babbling as usual, this time the "bus" refrain: "I like the bus, you like the bus, this one's a new bus." About the bus's relative age, at least, he was correct, since Market Town's city council finally made the decision to replace the aging fleet with smaller, more efficient vehicles that ran on compressed natural gas. Progress had come late to Market Town, too late for Margaret to witness its effects.

Polly edged away from Slow Bo and wedged her backpack into a barrier between them. They passed a row of car dealerships, hotels where no one stayed unless it was football season, restaurants meant for families and old people on vacation, specialty stores selling everything for your pet, everything for your bathroom, everything for the party you're hosting to make up for the loneliness you feel after remodeling your bathroom and dressing up your pet. The recent efforts toward urban revitalization seemed not to include grocery stores or gas stations—those remained hidden behind the main drag in what they called Old Town, funny since nothing in Oklahoma was much older than the so-called Land Run of the late nineteenth century, the mad grab for bargain basement homesteads in which the victors, also the cheaters, made a mockery of the spoils.

That day, Polly had her "smart" phone with her—she was catching up on the news—and, sick as she was of Slow Bo's repetitive proclamations, she made the mistake of telling him about the First Dog's brush with disaster during the third-grade field trip to the White House.

"Bo Bama *bites*?" Slow Bo said.

"Almost," Polly said. "Everything worked out fine, though."

"I'm scared of Bo Bama."

"Oh, I don't think he's that scary."

"Bo Bama bites!"

"He didn't bite anyone."

"You still like Bo Bama?"

"Sure."

"Me and her like Bo Bama," he told the driver for perhaps the thirtieth time. The driver, exercising his usual phony deafness, said nothing, but pulled in for his usual stop at the bus depot, a ten-minute wait while he went inside for a cup of coffee. Sometimes a different driver would return, sometimes the same one, but either way he was surly. This time, the same driver returned and wordlessly resumed the humming monotony of the trip through Market Town. Just as they were making the slow turn into the Student Union parking lot, two things happened: another e-mail from Margaret arrived on Polly's smart phone, and Polly lost another tooth, her second in as many weeks.

Polly, the e-mail said. *Despite what you may have heard, Abraham Lincoln was not gay. Neither does our current president have a secret longing for Oprah Winfrey. Still, the cherry blossoms are in bloom, and my thoughts are with you. Did I ever tell you about Geoffrey's last asthma attack? The two of us were reading magazines in the emergency room, waiting for what seemed like hours beneath an unbearable television set, when who should walk through the automatic sliding doors but a young, tattooed couple, the man without a shirt and the woman wearing only a bathrobe. The palms of their hands, Polly, were superglued together; they'd done it on purpose, as a kind of commitment ceremony, but they were having regrets. I, too, am having these regrets. The question*

is, Polly, how did the doctor reverse the effects of the glue?
Don't bother, I already looked it up. Geoffrey sends his best.
You ought to visit sometime.

Again, Polly reeled with disbelief. The last e-mail she'd chalked up to her own careless, lovesick inebriation, but here she was, stone-cold sober, on the bus of all places, reading what appeared to be an authentic, even flirtatious missive from the person who consumed most of her waking thoughts. Out the window, the weeds waved in the wind and almost seemed like flowers, and the sky burst into a cloudless blue. The whole world blossomed and swayed, the scene resembling one she'd seen in a YouTube video of vibrant bicycle riders smiling and waving in the Netherlands of 1959. At work, while everyone else was in a staff meeting, she celebrated by ordering a case of Super Glue, three six-packs of rubber cement, and an unknown quantity of "grab bag" glue sticks. A joke, she thought, she'd send some of it to Margaret for her birthday. She was so consumed with the vision of Margaret's eventual return to Market Town, she almost forgot about her missing tooth, another wisdom tooth, she supposed, though this one, like the one before it, didn't hurt at all. Had it fallen out while she was eating lunch, she might have swallowed it by mistake.

Confident no one would notice the slight change in her appearance, she didn't bother to make a dentist's appointment. And no one did notice, or at least they didn't say so, until the next morning on the bus, when Slow Bo, just like clockwork, announced Polly's personal business to the other passengers.

"This girl's got a girlfriend," he said. Fortunately, no one paid him any mind. The other passengers' lack of attention angered him, though, so he repeated himself, the second time with added salacious details. "This toothless *girl* likes *girls*," he said. "She wants to kiss another girl. With her tongue." None of the other passengers much cared; still, Polly was annoyed enough to ask him where and how he thought he'd discovered this information. He said he could just tell.

"How can you tell?"

"You don't wear makeup," he said, an accurate observation, though Polly didn't realize the natural look gave so much away. "And you wear jeans," he said. "Every day." Also true, but did this make most American schoolchildren gay?

"We won't comment on the ambiguous nature of *your* sexuality," she said to Slow Bo, meanly. He knew enough to look insulted, but she had succeeded in disarming him, at least, and he changed tactics so that he turned to another passenger and began to point out fire hydrants out the window. For a while she considered his actions, finally rejecting the theory Slow Bo had become the manifestation of her unconscious mind. And how did he know she had lost another tooth? That night she wrote to Margaret in the safety of a spiral notebook—no chance she would accidentally hit "send" and embarrass herself for the ages. *Dear Margaret,* she wrote. *Tomorrow, I'm going to the dentist where I'm sure they'll offer to glue fake teeth into my mouth. I once had a dream in which I had a single tooth growing like a potato tuber behind my earlobe. And it hurt like hell. Please, Margaret, return to*

Market Town before I do something drastic like put this letter in an envelope and mail it to Washington. I miss you terribly and I cannot bear this place without you. Please write again. She ripped the letter from the notebook, folded it in thirds and then in half, and then, at a loss, into the back pocket of her jeans, where she would carry it around for the next two days.

On the third day, she rode the bus to work and decided to take out the letter and read it, for sentimental reasons, mostly, and because she'd left her smart phone charging at home. Ever since Polly's remark on his sexuality, Slow Bo had taken to sitting in the front of the bus, near the driver and as far as possible from Polly. His absence was a relief, though his newfound snobbery hurt her feelings too, since no one liked being excluded from a club, even if the club's only members were a slow-witted fast food worker and a fascist bus driver. Worse, the driver had taken to speaking to Bo in low tones, a conspiracy of fear and loathing punctuated by quick bursts of animation. Never before had Bo laughed at *her* jokes with so much urgency or energy. She contented herself only with the knowledge she would enjoy a peaceful bus ride, for once, and soothed herself further with the promise of writing another letter to Margaret during her lunch hour at work. But when she unfolded the wrinkled piece of notebook paper on which she had written her secret love letter, she discovered something strange had happened. Her own note had disappeared somehow—not a trace of it remained—and Margaret, against all odds and in opposition to every law of the Internet, postal mail, and the space-time continuum, had written back.

Dear Polly, the paper said in the handwriting Polly would recognize anywhere. *To find yourself in this city is to find yourself in hell. I hate to say it, but the grass is always greener. I'm writing to you out of necessity. Please: Geoffrey is away. Come.*

Here she imagined herself in the midst of a waking dream. Since when did entire handwritten paragraphs disappear? Or maybe she had neglected to remember playing a joke on herself, like the time she left a note to her future self in the pocket of her winter jacket when she put it away for spring. But the handwriting had all of Margaret's unmistakable flourishes, and the black ink—Margaret's black ink—streaked and puddled in the familiar way Polly had seen so many times on Margaret's legal pads at work. Once, she'd stolen one of Margaret's legal pads, notes on a deposition when a bicycle rider wedged her front tire in a neglected drainage grate, broke her leg, sued the City of Market Town, and, eventually, won. A sweet victory that had been, too, since Margaret seemed so cheered by the settlement amount she'd ordered brand new bicycles for everyone in the firm. And since the case was over, closed, Polly felt safe taking the legal pad home, a talisman, she thought, something to remind her of Margaret's intelligence. Later, something else had come up, another bicycle rider, injured when a city garbage truck turned too fast off the highway, and Margaret looked everywhere for her old notes. Polly felt guilty, but said nothing and never returned the legal pad. This was right around the same time she started ordering office supplies in massive quantities—a hundred cases of new, fresh clean legal pads to replace the single one she'd stolen. And it all seemed harmless enough until the day after Margaret's handwritten note appeared as if by magic in the back pocket of Polly's oh-so-lesbian jeans.

At work, she put the note in the top drawer of her desk. And she locked it, too, thinking the custodian, a man not unlike Slow Bo, had a nosy streak and might embarrass her in front of the rest of the firm. She spent the morning surfing the web for law schools with late deadlines for admission, and everything seemed to proceed more or less as usual until a police officer showed up at her desk and asked her if on February 14th—Valentine's Day!—she'd purchased nearly ten thousand dollars worth of office supplies at the local office super store, including three laser printers, a portable Xerox machine, four executive office chairs, a faux mahogany desk, and—here was the sticking point—more than two thousand dollars worth of push pins, thumb tacks, coffee filters, and dry erase markers. She was just stocking up, she insisted, but she knew she was sunk when the first cop radioed for a second cop, and together, the two of them unplugged and carted off Polly's computer, but not before taking what seemed like hundreds of digital photographs of the supply shelves lining the back wall of the law office. When the cops were gone and she went in to speak to her boss, his silence spoke volumes. She resisted the temptation to say, "Margaret at least would have had the guts to tell me I'm fired," and instead started on the slow, steady walk of shame back to her desk. Typically these scenarios allowed the shameful one to pack a cardboard box full of her possessions before sneaking off to the parking lot, but given the circumstances surrounding her forced resignation, she knew she had no choice but to walk out empty-handed. And so she did.

Though she wanted nothing more than to drink wine alone at home, she dutifully walked three blocks to her dentist's appointment where the dentist told her she had a Vitamin C deficiency, an impacted wisdom tooth—though the others had fallen out—and early-stage gum disease. They gave her laughing gas, two fillings, and another series of appointments that would total fifteen hundred dollars worth of cosmetic "tooth replacement," billable in easy monthly installments. The dentist sent her on her way, and finally, she took one step closer to putting an end to what was turning out to be the worst day of her adult life. She waited at the bus stop for a half an hour or more, and when the bus—big and orange as always—finally showed up and she climbed the steps to get on, she realized she didn't have the correct fare. She searched the depths of her purse, but the driver, silent and surly as always, waved her on for free. The bus was empty, but at the next stop—the so-called "new" Walmart—they picked up Slow Bo who was carrying, among other things, a plastic bag overflowing with hay.

"It's for my horse," he said. "He's hungry."

Polly said nothing in reply.

"You like Bo Bama?"

"Yes."

"'Cause I like Bo Bama."

"Sure."

"Those Obama girls need a horse."

"Giddy-up," she said. The laughing gas had yet to wear off, and, in a heady state of euphoria, she found herself thinking of the oddities of nineteenth-century medicine: the opium eaters, cocaine tooth drops, Fletcherism, the water cure.

Slow Bo poked her shoulder with his big, meaty finger and said, "You want to go there?"

Feeling faint, she said, "Where?"

"Bo Bama's house!"

"The White House?"

"Bo Bama's big white house."

Just then, the driver pulled into the bus depot and killed the engine. Polly watched as he lumbered down the steps and disappeared into the Big Orange Break Room. A short ten minutes would pass before his return, time enough for Bo to get hold of himself and become interested once again in the silence of his own thoughts.

"Let's go," Bo said. "I'll have my friend feed my horse while we're gone. We'll give this hay to those Bo-bama girls. Maybe their parents will buy them a horse."

She brushed him off with her usual promise to indulge him "some other time," but he would have nothing of it, his volume rising and his stride heavy with determination as he started down the aisle toward the driver's seat. Nothing to lose, he shouted with full-throated sincerity, and she realized he might have been speaking on her behalf, since she could think of no reason to remain in Market Town, not now, and, she'd always dreamed herself dangerous, always wished herself free. She thought of a cartoon she'd once seen in which a woman ran off to get married, tossing out the window to her waiting groom "everything but the kitchen sink," and, as an afterthought, the kitchen sink itself. She and Bo would have nothing but a few groceries and a bag full of hay. And the cops hot on their trail.

"Let me drive," she said.

"You drive us to the White House?"

"Yes," she said. She took her place in the driver's seat. Her fingers grazed the keys left carelessly in the ignition.

"For love?" he said.

"Yes," she said, and they were on their way.

Bun in the Oven

My old friend Eleanor was getting a divorce. A long time ago, before they were married, I lived with Eleanor and Stan and a bunch of other people in a four-bedroom house owned by the college Eleanor and I attended. Stan was much older, old enough to be considered scandalous, and we kept it under wraps he was living there at all. But he was gentle, the kind of man who played the acoustic guitar and volunteered to cook. These days, they lived in the mountains with their two sons, in a cabin heated only by a wood-burning stove. I was dying to know what had precipitated their divorce.

"What happened to Stan?" I said. We were in a bookstore, in the weirdo section, the two of us keeping company with healing aromas and Dr. Weil and crystals and mushrooms and shit. Eleanor was always a big believer in this or that. I was a doubter. The clash between her made-up mysticism and my unwelcome mockery was, in my mind, one of the most enjoyable parts of our friendship.

"Stan suffers from multiple addictions," she said. I thought multiple must have meant more than two. Probably he drank a lot and smoked pot and looked at pornography most of the time when he wasn't at work. Gambling seemed out of character, not to mention strangely anachronistic as addictions went. Maybe he wanted to have too much sex or did something extra-weird like buy too many bongo drums or drink too much cough medicine or make out with strangers in bathroom stalls. Or maybe he took pills. But I'll admit to disliking the language of addiction and 12-step programs; it seemed a bit pedestrian for someone as adventurous as Eleanor. I wanted to know what he'd done *to her*.

"When did you know?" I said. "Describe the exact moment."

"We were working in the garden," she said, "And he fell asleep under a tree."

"Yeah," I said. I could imagine the scene: a row of seedlings waiting to be planted, the boys off catching frogs in the creek, Eleanor up to her elbows in loose tree roots and dirt. His indifference, her loneliness, the boys being boys.

"You ought to buy this," I said, pointing to a display copy of *Stuff Your Pillows with Human Hair*. "Just kidding."

"I couldn't take it anymore," she said, and, in a flash, I remembered something that had happened years ago, when we all lived together in the college-owned house. One of our housemates, a six-foot-something woman from Buffalo, brought home a pizza and didn't share it with the rest of us. "You're a big eater," Stan had said to her. "Bun in the oven?" And at that moment, I'd watched as Eleanor looked at him and said silently, *I do not love you I cannot love you I will not love you.*

She had the same look now, only brighter, and more full of ease.

Remarkable

When I was nine years old, I watched my grandfather burn down the family business, a home furnishings store called Remarkable Lamps. Arson, I suppose you'd call it, though he hardly cared about the insurance money. Looking back, I can see how the pressure was getting to him. I don't think he woke up that morning thinking about the stack of tea towels he would toss in the trunk of his car and later use to douse in gasoline, but still, the evening ended in flames.

It was Halloween. Earlier that night, after trick-or-treating, but before bedtime, my grandfather wheeled the television set into the kitchen and the three of us shared a bowl of popcorn at the kitchen table. I was still dressed in my spider costume—a black leotard, wool tights, and a knotty, handmade mess of black yarn hanging off both my arms—when my grandmother, tired from a day spent cooking, found a diamond ring hidden among the apples and Hershey bars at the bottom of my Halloween goody bag.

"This is an omen," she said, dropping the apples into the trash.

Her kitchen glowed with celestial gloom. Silken

draperies closed against the neighborhood outside. Decorative plates hung on the walls, and a shelf in the front window housed a collection of colored glass. My grandfather sat at the table drinking coffee from a porcelain cup.

Grandmother shoveled the remaining Halloween candy into the door of the refrigerator, took up a paring knife, and began to slice at the mass of tangled yarn hanging off the arms of my spider costume.

"Watch out," my grandfather said. "You'll cut off the poor child's arm."

Everyone called me the poor child. The poor child looks like skin and bones. The poor child ought to learn some manners. The poor child needs a brother or sister. That I could do eighth grade algebra and play a mean violin never seemed to convince anyone that fortune, the kind that could be measured by handshakes and eye contact, would ever cast its light upon my sickly frame.

"She looks like a harlot," my grandmother said, still hacking away at the web of yarn. "You didn't even make her wear a coat."

"The weather, my dear, is balmy," Grandfather said. "And what with the neighbors giving out diamond rings and everything, I thought we should be showing off her costume. Stand up, Judith, show Grandma the way you catch flies in your web."

My grandfather, who wore a bow tie every day of the year except for Christmas, had the starved look of a specter rattling chains. Had he played a musical instrument, he would have played the pipe organ or bassoon.

I leaned forward in my chair, but my grandmother, her arm muscled from years spent working in the garden, pushed me down again and slammed the paring knife, blade facing my grandfather, onto the center crease in the kitchen table. Grandfather jumped.

"I'm serious," Grandmother said. "People don't just hand out diamond rings for Halloween. This is a sign."

Grandfather turned to me and said, "Go to bed, Judith." Then, to my grandmother, "The poor child never gets any sleep."

"I don't want to go to bed."

Grandmother grabbed a Baby Ruth from my goody bag and shook it at Grandfather. "I said this business decision of yours would bring us to ruin, and I was right."

The business decision, to hand over the day-to-day business of Remarkable Lamps to my father and stepmother, had caused its share of controversy, both within the family and without. Earlier that day, I had overheard my father and stepmother discussing selling off all the old merchandise and transforming the failing furniture store into a mail-order outlet for fake flowers and novelty gift items. They wanted to change the name to "A Bright Idea." Grandfather, powerless to stop them, would be crushed when he found out.

"Relax, Markie," Grandfather said. Markie was short for Remarkable, my grandmother's odd and beautiful first name. Remarkable Andrews Bradwardine. Grandfather named the furniture store after her.

"Take it back," Grandmother said. "Get Judith's coat and go back out. I'll wrap the ring in tissue paper."

"It's after ten o'clock," he said. "Listen to yourself."

"My costume is ruined," I said, happy to take Grandfather's side. "I can't go back out now."

So often my grandparents fell into these argument-driven, bizarre late night eruptions. Their neighbors, bankers and lawyers who rode their bicycles around the city square, witnessed their twilight fights on the tennis courts of the country club. Behind their backs, their bridge partners called them Calamity Jane and Frankenstein's monster. Worst of all, working in retail turned them half-crazy near the holidays. Blue light special! Lamps, lamps, lamps! Buy one get one free!

Finally, Grandfather agreed to go searching for the diamond ring's rightful owner: a newly engaged schoolteacher perhaps, or a doctor's wife whose weight loss program had made her finger too small for her former body's jewelry.

"Just start knocking on doors," Grandmother said. "Don't come back until you've rid the house of this curse."

Grandfather agreed, with the stipulation we would venture out in his Chevy rather than setting out on foot. On the way out the front door, he grabbed a stack of tea towels from behind the kitchen sink.

I always liked riding in my grandfather's car. To this day, the smell of pipe tobacco makes me think of the soft glow from the interior dome light, the tall black dashboard, the polished chrome on the radio's oversized dials.

"Hop in," my grandfather said, patting the passenger seat as if ushering a pet toward a dreaded visit to the vet's office. "We'll make a few passes around the block, and, by the time we come back, she'll have forgotten all about us. That woman's attention span is shorter than a five-cent fuse."

I slid into the front seat and relaxed into the dark cave of the car. Grandfather tuned the radio until he found a weather report and slowly backed out of the long gravel driveway. In an instant, he reached for a flask he kept tucked in the breast pocket of his jacket and took a long swig. The diamond ring, safe in its cocoon of tissue paper, seemed somehow dangerous on the front seat between us.

"My costume," I said. "No one can see it under this coat."

"Don't worry," he said, swallowing hard from the flask. "The coat is only for show. You can take it off as soon as we go around the corner here."

He put on his blinker and turned without slowing down. Crossing the center line, he veered into the oncoming traffic, but pulled back again at the last minute. In those days before Mothers Against Drunk Driving, mothers (and fathers, too) could do most anything they pleased. I took off my coat and threw it onto the backseat. Pleased with Grandfather's plan to orchestrate some small, secret deception, I patted him on the shoulder.

Soon, we found ourselves heading toward the commercial district, the tall trees of my grandparents' country club neighborhood disappearing into the distance. I didn't yet know how to find my way around town, but I instinctually knew my own house lay somewhere ahead, a long ride past a winding brick lane with churches on either side. My elementary school and the grocery store were further still.

Finally, I realized we were heading toward the grand brick building formerly known as Remarkable Lamps. My grandfather's thumbs tapped against the steering wheel as we cruised past the shutter mill, the pipe fitters' warehouse, and the typewriter repair shop. I didn't understand the full extent of his anger, but knew full well my father's newfound fortune came at the expense of Grandfather's giving in to old age. Grandfather's was the land of obsolescence, the fact of hard work's forgotten promise, and the final, heart-stopping reality of depression and debt.

Maybe he drove to Remarkable Lamps because he always did, because his daily commute seemed like the only habit worth repeating, because his Chevy knew no other destination. At the time, I thought he wanted only to make quick work of the diamond ring, and, wise with the knowledge his wife, Remarkable Andrews Bradwardine, would vow never to set foot on the premises of the failed family business, he figured Remarkable's dumpster was the only place safe from its namesake's prying eyes.

"Listen," he said, stopping the car in front of a series of wooden crates stacked up around the edges of Remarkable's loading dock. He turned off the headlights. "Don't tell your grandmother. We're going to leave the diamond ring for the garbage men. No one will know the difference."

"She'll find out," I said. I fiddled with the black yarn on my costume. "We had better go back to the Country Club and start knocking on doors."

"Going soft on me, are you?"

"No," I said. "She'll be angry."

"I'll worry about that," he said. "Stay here."

With a quick, one-handed motion, he grabbed the wad of tissue paper containing the diamond ring and stuffed the slim crinkled packet into his closed fist. He left the car running and the driver's seat door open. In an instant, I heard the clank of diamond against dumpster-bottom metal. I hadn't known the dumpster would be empty. He, too, seemed surprised the garbage truck already had come and gone.

"No one ever tells me what's happening around here," he said when he returned. "Used to be Mondays and Thursdays."

"Someone will find it," I said. "We'll get in trouble."

He turned on the car's headlights. The loading dock, flattened cardboard boxes stacked in every corner, shone under the twin round beams. Broken basement windows allowed feral cats to deposit their kittens in the warm confines of Remarkable's old location for first-floor electrical storage. A metal sign ordering employees to park in the rear of the building, one of my father's crowd control initiatives, leaned to one side, its lettering splattered with mud. Curtains hanging in Remarkable's executive office suite looked thin like my grandfather's eyelids right before bed.

"Listen," he said. "Did you, or did you not, find that diamond ring in the bottom of your Halloween goody bag?"

"I did."

"And are you, or are you not, under my care and protection for the next forty-eight hours at least?"

"Until my dad gets back, I guess."

"Your dad," he said. "Someday you'll understand about him."

"He wants to change the name," I said, impulsively, knowing this revelation would hurt him. "He wants to call it, A Bright Idea."

The color in his face changed—a dramatic darkening like lights in a stage play. He put the Chevy in reverse and backed away from the loading dock.

I wanted something to happen. And I wanted to feel important. Whether my actions arose from cruelty or mere curiosity, I do not know. In any case, I turned to my grandfather and said, "He's changing everything. He wants to sell off all the furniture and buy a bunch of whoopee cushions and fake flowers and plastic dog poop and—"

"Enough," he said, then, immediately, "When did he decide this?"

"I don't know," I said. "Can we go home?"

"In a minute," he said. "Put on your coat."

By then, I knew for sure my costume would garner no more admiring looks that Halloween night, so I did as he suggested and fumbled in the backseat for my parka. Resentful, I zipped up the front and drew the hood around my head.

"Listen, Judith," he said. "One day you're going to grow up and some handsome young fellow is going to have his own bright idea and give you one of those diamond rings for real. He'll control the money and you'll have nothing but his good graces at allowance time. Don't fall back on your savings. Get a job."

At the time, I thought I wanted to be a veterinarian,

so I heartily agreed with his admonition.

"A bright idea," he said again. "Whoever heard of such a thing?"

If Remarkable Lamps meant hard work and continual worry, A Bright Idea might mean instant profits and customers crowding the showroom floor. Not that my grandfather cared. I didn't know anything about business, but I did have that strange sense of entitlement so many young people possess, the same robust awareness that leads children to order their parents to stop smoking or to mock their grandparents' taste in music. Marketers target children and children aren't stupid. Always they carry with them the knowledge of their own superiority. For my money, a pack of chewing gum that would stain your tongue an inky black sounded better than a sectional sofa any day of the week. So it would not have bothered me to see Remarkable Lamps become a wasteland of plastic crap made in China—nowadays, most furniture, too, is plastic crap made in China—but I knew Grandfather had put his entire life into making the furniture store successful. Plus, I wanted someone to notice me. I don't know what my grandfather wanted. Maybe old age found him retreating into childhood and he, too, wanted the barest measure of respect.

I've never told anyone this before, but we did it together. Together, we burned down Remarkable Lamps. Together in the front seat of his Chevy, we hatched our plans. The clock struck eleven—I counted the low, sonorous tones from the bank building nearby. For a while, we said nothing. I opened and closed the glove box; he drank from his flask. He asked me if I remembered the bonfire at the beach last Fourth of July. Of course, I said, how could I forget? He asked me if I had enjoyed myself, and I assured him I'd had loads of fun, the bonfire and the fireworks later on had been my favorite parts of the whole weekend. What if, he said, we made a practice of having bonfires on every major holiday—Christmas, New Year's, my birthday, and especially and most importantly, Halloween. We needed to show people, he said. We needed to show people we were people of action.

"I'm a person of action," I said.

"Of course you are."

"Who cares about a bunch of nasty old furniture, anyway," I said.

"You're right," he said. "It's worthless."

He parked the car underneath a streetlamp about a block away. In the distance, we could hear music— disco? rock 'n' roll?—blaring from some faraway Halloween party in the college district down the block. The downtown streets, though, were all but empty. In the trunk of his car, he had a can of gasoline, a box of matches, and the stack of tea towels he had grabbed from behind the kitchen sink. We walked along together past the shuttered stores. He carried the matches and tea towels; I carried the gas.

By the time we made it to the loading dock, Grandfather was out of breath. One last chore, he said, and then we'd be able to have some real fun. We deposited our fire-starting tools underneath an awning by the service entrance and returned empty-handed to the loading dock. Quietly, we approached the metal dumpster, empty except for the diamond ring wrapped in tissue paper. He stacked up two empty crates against the side of the dumpster and climbed on top of the leaning tower. A mistake, he said. Throwing away the diamond ring had been a terrible mistake. I asked him how we could possibly get it back, and he explained his plan to hold me by the ankles and lower me down into the dumpster. At first, I was afraid. His grip, I knew, was not the firmest, and I shuddered to think about Grandmother's reaction upon discovering he had deposited me in a dumpster and left me alone to die. Finally, he convinced me of the merits of his plan, and I stacked two additional wooden crates and climbed up toward my grandfather who, birdlike, perched above me on the edge of his own makeshift platform.

I scooted up, the wool on my costume snagging the roughness on the wooden crates. The front face of the dumpster angled down toward the parking lot in a slight slope, so I could lean toward the outer edge without falling to the bottom. Grandfather gripped my waist, and I reached toward the darkness below. To my surprise, the dumpster was not empty at all, rather tall stacks of sofa cushions leaned on either side of the wad of paper I assumed to contain the diamond ring. Grandfather coaxed me forward. I groped through the darkness and tried not to inhale the stench of a thousand moldy carpet samples and the forgotten banana peels from thirty years' worth of discarded bag lunches. Finally, my hands greasy and my costume ripped, I emerged from the dumpster victorious.

"The diamond ring," I said. "I'm rich."

We stepped down from our wooden crates and felt ourselves once again on firm ground. Grandfather unwrapped the diamond ring and placed it on my finger, though it was too large for me by far. I cupped the ring in the palm of my hand. He knelt, taking my hand in his.

"Judith," he said. "This is important."

"We should go home."

"Keep this ring," he said. "It's yours. Forever."

"Grandmother will find out. Dad will find out."

He assured me the secret would be ours. I put the diamond ring in the front pocket of my parka. For the remainder of my childhood, I kept the ring in the far reaches of my closet, the crinkle of tissue paper every year during spring cleaning a reminder of my hidden shame. After graduating high school, I moved the ring to a safe deposit box in the local post office—a secret, even from those closest to me. For a while, I imagined I would give it to my own daughter on her wedding day, but my daughter, I can already tell, will not marry. Maybe all the more reason to give her the ring.

I think Grandfather wanted to hurt my father. Or he wanted to determine his furniture store's fate: never would it stoop to the level of hucksterism. Probably, too, he wanted to hurt my grandmother, to steal the furniture store from her for good. Why he made me his accomplice I don't know. In any case, I was a willing conspirator.

We walked back to the service entrance where he instructed me to stuff the tea towels in various strategic locations—in the door jambs, between the gutters and the wooden shingles around the facing of the service entrance, in the open window of first-floor electrical storage. He did his own work quickly and efficiently, the fumes from the gas burning both our eyes. I felt excited, the same way I might feel during a tornado warning or upon learning of a snow day from school. He ordered me to stand back.

"Some things aren't worth saving," he said.

"I know."

"This is the right thing to do."

"I know."

"Remarkable," he said, and lit the first match.

The Love Feast

Long before the swimming party that resulted in my arrest, my wife claimed to know there was something wrong with me, a screw loose, she said, a biological blunder. So what if I'd meant well? Didn't matter in her book. But ever since her doctor prescribed an antipsychotic after she confessed to losing interest in her previous passion for finding forever-homes for stray dogs and cats, she'd had a tendency to pathologize—not my fault. Our next-door neighbors, Barry and Doughboy, community college dropouts who practiced with their garage band at all hours of the night, also suffered under her diagnostic gaze. My proposed solution to their nightly jam sessions was either to pound on their basement window with a broomstick or give the cops a call, but my wife said Doughboy had a chemical imbalance; he couldn't help it. She said the same thing when my birthday cake came back from the grocery store's bakery with American flags and "Happy Birthday, U.S.A." written on it. The cake decorator, she said, had "brain trouble," a stripped wire or a gear gone wrong. You know those commercials where the diamond-shaped white pills turn into miniaturized socket wrench sets as soon as they enter the animated human bloodstream? Those commercials were meant for her.

Still, she might have been right to suggest there was something wrong with me. Our daughter was off to college and I'd been staying up late washing and drying all the clothes she'd left behind in the basement. After her acrylic sweaters came out shrunken and hot from the dryer, I'd put them back in the washer and start all over again. And I couldn't stop watering the crepe myrtle she'd planted in the front yard. You might say I overwatered it. When the mud puddle at the end of the gravel driveway grew large enough to threaten the mailman's steady gait from house to house, I felt so guilty I tried to make up for it by running an extension cord from the garage and firing up the dehumidifier at odd hours. I put it on low, but still: Barry and Doughboy thought I was nuts.

In any case, I missed my daughter, and perhaps the thing that made me miss her the most was the swimming pool in our backyard. I didn't know how to swim, and my wife knew only how to dog paddle, enough, she said to rescue me if I ever slipped and fell. My fear of drowning was compounded by our daughter's absence, since she'd left home just weeks before for the University of Oklahoma on a swimming scholarship. Before she left, she was a lifeguard at the city pool, an expert at saving lives. When she was sixteen, she strapped a kid to one of those wooden boards and kept him from paralysis. His parents ended up suing the City and winning a handsome settlement, but still: my daughter gave that kid his legs back. To this day, whenever I see him walking around the vitamin supplement section at Walmart or jogging the neighborhood streets, I give him the thumbs-up. He always tries to look away, but I know the score.

All this is to say I'd been a little crazy since my daughter moved out. It might have been different if I had a son, but I do not. At the time, I didn't even have a dog. My wife, in spite of all her previous claims on behalf of the Humane Society, wouldn't allow them in the house. She said dogs and cats both were "triggers" for her. I said triggers for what and she said I would never understand, so what was the point in trying? That's when I told her I was going to start volunteering by serving soup at the Section 8 housing addition south of town. She said they didn't serve soup in the summertime, and I said I didn't care, I'd serve them biscuits from a can if it meant I'd be able to get away from her. She said biscuits from a can were actually very good these days, and she didn't mind at all if I found some hobbies for a change, and that I should not wear one of my golf shirts on community dinner nights because they'd think I was an elitist.

"That's my casual wear," I said, the truth. "All my T-shirts are white."

She said it was about time I bought some new T-shirts anyway—and maybe she had a point—so we loaded all the recycled cans I'd been saving up into the back of her minivan, cashed them in at the scrap metal yard, and felt suddenly rich enough to go to JCPenney, not my favorite place, but better than Walmart, better than Goodwill.

And wouldn't you know it, Barry, of Barry and Doughboy fame, actually *worked* at JCPenney? He'd never mentioned it before.

"Mr. and Mrs. Gildersleve," he said. "Back to school shopping?"

"Don't joke with me, Barry," I said.

My wife put her hand on my wrist—something she never did at home—and complimented Barry on his nice, broad forehead. Now let's get something straight: after everything was said and done, I realized my judgment was off. You might even say I was suffering under some heavy-duty delusions. But one thing I know I was right about was Barry's appearance. He did *not* have a nice, broad forehead. Broad, maybe, but definitely not nice. And though he was twenty years old if he was a day, he had a receding hairline and walked with a limp. At this point, you're thinking cancer victim or golf injury or something, but really, he was just a weird guy, which, I suppose, made me feel more attractive by comparison, but jeez, it wasn't my fault.

Finally, Barry pointed us in the direction of men's wear—how he knew we were shopping for me and not my wife I'll never know—and I felt more or less free to browse the racks for new, colorful, casual shirts in a wide variety of styles. But he kept showing up out of nowhere to fold nearby stacks of swimsuits or sweep imaginary crumbs from the carpet near the dressing room. I know he worked there and everything, and his job was to appear busy when the boss decided to spy on him, but I could not escape the feeling he was following me. When I said as much to my wife, she replied only to say I was paranoid, after which she admonished me not to speak for fear he might overhear.

"That's just what I'm talking about," I said. "He's eavesdropping."

"Don't be ridiculous."

"I'm not," I said. I removed a glittering gold T-shirt from its hanger, held it up to my chest, and took a stance similar to the ones you see referees make as overdramatized reactions to instant replays during televised sporting events. "Hey, Barry! Over here, buddy."

"That shirt's on sale," Barry said. "Looks good."

"You think I could wear this golfing?"

"Sure," he said. "Why not?"

"You ever golf, Barry?"

"Not since the accident," he said.

My wife turned to me and gave me a pleading look, *shut up*, said her eyes. *I would do anything if you would just please shut up.* I gave in.

"I understand," I said. "I'll take this shirt and one in red while you're at it. I'm going to wear these to the soup kitchen."

And here was when I knew my wife was cheating on me, and she was doing it with Barry: "They don't serve soup in the summertime," he said. "You might try biscuits from a can."

Later, in the minivan on the way home, my wife insisted Barry's knowledge of my charitable activities was just a coincidence. And biscuits from a can? Anybody could mention biscuits from a can for any reason at all.

Now I don't like to be nasty. And I'm well-aware people who say things like, "I don't like to be nasty" are usually the first ones to stab you in the back, but I'll tell you, I'm an upstanding guy. I was not the kind of person to compare our marital love life to biscuits in a can, but if I were, I would have said something like *you think you're hot snot on a silver platter, but you're really a cold biscuit on a paper plate.* I learned that expression from my daughter when she was much younger, and the correct euphemism is cold *booger* on a paper plate, but you get the idea: though my wife had read a lot of articles instructing women on the finer points of putting the spice back in their marriages, her idea of spice was more like Mrs. Dash. If your spice rack has never seen the likes of Mrs. Dash you don't know what I'm talking about, but trust me, it is nothing special.

Something my wife didn't know was that Barry and Doughboy called me Numb-nuts when they thought I wasn't around. Those knuckleheads? Calling *me* Numb-nuts? You'd have to see them to know what I'm talking about. I played golf, for one thing, and Barry and Doughboy were more the types to try to steal the golf cart than to stick it out for a full eighteen holes. Between Barry's limp and Doughboy's chemical imbalance I could have been Mr. America or at least Mr. Oklahoma Coupon-Clipper House Husband Helper. Because even though my wife complained about me incessantly, she didn't know how lucky she had it, since I saved us at least a hundred bucks a month on groceries and did all the laundry, even when it didn't need doing, and I took such good care of the yard we could have appeared in *House Beautiful*, if editors of magazines like that ever came to Oklahoma, which they did not, so I'll just say my yard looked almost as good as a golf course except with more flowers.

The day after our trip to JCPenney, my wife said she was sick of men sitting with their legs spread out, as if they always needed to air out their balls. I wasn't even sitting like that, so I'm not sure why she chose that exact moment to complain about the men who took up too much room on the bus or the subway, not that we had subways in Oklahoma, because we did not. So what was the big deal, anyway?

Here we were, sitting across from one another in the breakfast nook, companionably eating scrambled eggs that *I had made*, when bam, she hit me with this men-need-to-act-better crap. At the time, I thought, though I realize now I was in error, she was merely trying to distract me from the certain knowledge of her affair with Barry.

"He's a kid, Paul," she said. "I'm old enough to be his mother."

"I've seen *The Graduate*," I said. "I've seen *Animal House*."

"Nothing like that happens in *Animal House*, so you can take your movie collection and sell it in a garage sale."

My movie collection was a touchy subject between my wife and me. I'd been copying—I guess you could call it pirating—all the new releases since the days of the Betamax and so had in my possession more or less every movie that had appeared in mainstream release since 1985, though I never spoke about it outside our house for fear of listening devices from the FBI. Buried in the subtext of our public appearances together was the constant implication any real or imagined offense on my part would allow her license to turn me in. *Ever seen The Sound of Music,* she'd say to me at cocktail parties and weddings. *Oh yes, Paul owns a copy and we watch it all the time. The Hills are alive, aren't they Paul, with the Sound of Music?* To say I was running scared would be an overstatement, but I knew she wouldn't hesitate to buy a couple of boxes of lawn and leaf trash bags and have my entire collection on the curb if ever I made one wrong move in terms of what she called her core values, *compassion* being number one on the list and *communication* being number two.

I decided to take a bus for my first visit to the Section 8 Housing south of town. When the people who actually *live* in Section 8 Housing—Southern Heights, they call it—have to come into town for groceries or to go to JCPenney, *they* have to take a bus—none of them have cars to speak of—so I thought I ought to try to blend in. My wife wanted me to wear a T-shirt so as to appear more modern, but the truth is, and I'm not even sure how to put this, exactly, but the truth is about 95% of the people who live in Southern Heights are African American, and the other 5% might as well be. Probably you've figured out by now I'm white. And I'm not just regular-old peaches 'n' cream. I'm white as your proverbial ghost, a regular pasty-faced doughboy, maybe not as doughy as our neighbor, Doughboy, though I'm probably whiter than him by far. So I was nervous, heading out that day on the bus, my first day serving biscuits at Southern Heights. I'd chosen an off-hour and so was the only passenger, seated as I was in the front seat right behind the driver, who, I might add, was not African American and not white but Indian, as in from India, not the reservation casino. I'm not sure what he was doing in Oklahoma, but probably going to community college or engineering us all to our nuclear doom.

"Off to Southern Heights?" he said, when he realized I'd chosen to remain on the bus past the highway roadhouse called Mom's Diner, past the Harley-Davidson place, past the Town & Gown Community Theater.

"Yeah," I said. "I go there all the time."

"Let me guess," he said, with that annoying English accent Indian people have. "Your church sponsors you."

Here I pretended to be mortally offended. "My *church*?" I said. "I don't need a *church* to tell me I ought to try to *help* people."

"Oh yeah," he said. "I know your type. Biscuits from a can, right?"

How did he know? I began to suspect one of Barry's practical jokes or some elaborate surveillance scheme on the part of my wife. And it's not like I had any biscuits or really any food at all in my possession, since I was going to Southern Heights, that first day, only to get the lay of the land. But I'd been reading about consumer demographics in *US News & World Report* and figured this smarty-pants bus driver had been doing the same.

"It's nothing," he said, in what I assumed was an attempt to reassure me. "I know what Oklahomans consider *home cooking*, that's all."

"Are we almost there?" I said. "Because this bus is making me *hot*."

"You're going to love Southern Heights," he said. "Very pleasant, very temperate. The children push one another around in a trolley."

It turned out he was talking about an old, rusty shopping cart with a bum wheel and a handle taped together with what they call "Oklahoma gold," the ubiquitous silver duct tape. And indeed the children seemed to be having a good time, there in the noisy chaos of the playground, which, now that I think about it, wasn't so much a playground as it was a concrete slab with a sandy fringe of dead leaves and scattered trash like rusty bottle caps and loose bits of those plastic collars from gallons of milk. They had twin basketball goals, lowered to make it easier, but the nets had been replaced with greasy metal chains that made a clanging sound in the wind. Interested, as they were, in what seemed to be an elaborate dodge ball/capture-the-flag hybrid involving the periodic dumping of a lesser individual from the shopping cart onto a weedy patch of grass, they seemed not to notice my arrival, or, if they did, they kept it to themselves.

"Hi," I said to a tall boy, about twelve. "I'm here for the Love Feast."

"They don't call it that anymore," he said, pointing to a large outbuilding that looked to me like a 1970s golf pro shop, overtaken by ivy not quite poisoned and not quite benevolent, full of faded curtains and faded grandeur, a country club gone to seed. "It's in there."

I waved to the rest of the children, friendly little tykes who, I might add, did indeed wave back with more than the usual level of interest and appreciation. "I'm looking for the Love Feast," I said to the first white person I saw, an elderly man wearing a golf shirt very much like the ones I had at home. "I'm aware they don't call it the Love Feast anymore," I said. "But I'd like to help."

The elderly white man, it turned out, was in charge of games and recreation, an easy job, I thought, suitable for someone with lesser talents than the ones I knew I possessed peeling potatoes or baking pie crusts in what I imagined was a cavernous industrial kitchen. And judging from the shopping cart games still in progress, he wasn't doing a very good job, and don't give me that "all volunteers are good volunteers" crap, either, because even at that early date I knew the score. He looked to me like a Methodist, or maybe a Presbyterian, and I was neither. You had to watch out for the Unitarians, though; they could fool you. At any time they'd welcome you to some discount sale for eco-friendly sandals or free-thinkers' book club and you'd be stuck there for the rest of your life.

"No dinner tonight," the elderly "recreation leader" said. "Someone's bringing in pizzas and crazy bread. Later on."

"Doesn't sound very nutritious," I said. "These are growing children."

By this time, the shopping cart game had reached its noisy conclusion, the result of boredom or fatigue or maybe injury, since I couldn't help but notice one boy, a small one about seven or eight, was clutching his leg in pain. The dead leaves on the playground swirled into a pile, and the sky above darkened with the threat of rain. I wanted some pizza. I could skip the crazy bread, but I began to worry whoever placed the order might not have accounted for as many adults as were actually present. Would I end up stealing a slice from a child? Anything was possible; desperation might have driven me to worse.

"If they don't call it the Love Feast," I said to the elderly recreation leader, "What do they call it?"

"We're still working on that," he said. He stuck his thumb back toward the dilapidated outbuilding. "You can vote in there if you want."

It was at that exact moment I began to think of my daughter off in college. I missed her terribly. Maybe my wife was right, I had some sort of chemical imbalance, the four humors flowing through my bloodstream mixing into some kind of evil witches' brew and spewing forth in the form of my wretched saliva. I began to cough uncontrollably.

"You all right?" the elderly man said. "Take it easy there, fellow."

I did not tell him about my daughter, about the way she did her laundry every Saturday morning before the sun came up, about the ink barely dry on her swimming scholarship, about the way she leaned in at the dinner table and called me Pops. Instead, I made up some phony excuse about needing a drink of water, or maybe some lemonade if they had it, and followed him in through the smudged glass doors of the outbuilding. When the pizzas finally arrived, I ended up stuck with some crappy vegetarian option, my customary four slices diminished to a more tasteful and respectful two.

"I'm leaving my wife," I told the recreation leader guy.

I didn't even know his name. We sat there, together on a low bench overlooking the playground, our stomachs rumbling from hunger. Two slim pieces of some kind of green pepper mushroom thing was just not enough.

"We get a lot of that kind of thing out here," he said. "Men leaving their wives."

"Wives leaving their husbands?" I said. "You get any of that?"

"Nah," he said. "They're into dogs and cats."

"Yeah," I said. "That's my wife all over the place."

We sat there watching the children kick a soccer ball into the fence. It appeared to me they were playing another game of their own invention, a timed sequence of events with an elaborate and color-coded scoring system. They yelled colors and numbers, advice to the smaller ones, and congratulations to successful shooters, but there was a surprising absence of bad sportsmanship, since it appeared to me also this particular game did not have winners and losers but only continued on until the next day. That's when I had the idea to invite them over for a swimming party.

"Absolutely not," my wife said, later that evening over a bowl of popcorn at home. "One of them might drown. Think about our insurance, Paul."

"They're excellent swimmers," I said. "I can tell."

"Who's going to rescue them," she said, laughing and stuffing her face. "You?"

"Give me some of that popcorn," I said. "I'm starved."

In the end, reason and charity won over hostility and fear. We planned the party for the Fourth of July weekend, a stretch of leisurely days during which

I knew my daughter would come home to do her laundry. In preparation, I washed and dried all my clothes, my wife's, and all the sheets, towels, and kitchen dishcloths. I hired Barry and Doughboy to clean the leaves from the swimming pool and rinse out the filter. And I decorated: little crystal light bulbs with red, white, and blue streamers trailing off the ends. Something in me knew this most American of American holidays would bring us all together in peace.

I did not go back to the Love Feast. Since my first visit, however, I'd been working on coming up with an alternative name, something like The Sinner Dinner or Eat Your Heart Out. I had in mind I would propose the best of my invented names over a toast—plastic stemware only—at the conclusion of the swimming party, a gathering, I was proud to announce, that would also feature at least half a medium pizza for every guest in attendance. We never made it to the toast *or* to the pizzas because my wife had me arrested before the refreshments came. When you hear about it you'll understand how stupid it was. The children were playing another one of their games—sort of like "Marco Polo," but refusing the well-known explorer in favor of the names of teen music sensations. My daughter had called just five minutes prior to the start of the party to announce she was going to do her laundry at a friend's house and then swim laps at the YMCA. I told her we'd welcome a professional swimmer at the swimming party, but she wouldn't hear of it. I knew this meant all my laundry chores had been for nothing.

I took a risk and jumped into the shallow end, the

water cold like a great idea. I heard my wife laughing on the sidelines. "Just like in that movie, *Cocoon*," she said. "You know, with the old people." I took a deep breath and dunked my head in the splendor of the chlorinated sensation of silence, imagining, in the privacy of the humming beauty of the skimmer's motor, a vision of myself rising from the deep with a mouthful of water, my cheeks like a chipmunk's until I found a way to propel the water in the direction of her smug little face. Barry and Doughboy were there, and their presence, I suppose, was my downfall. Doughboy challenged me to a race, and when I explained I didn't know how to swim, he modified the rules so that we remained in the shallow end and competed in a furious walk-splash-dog-paddle combination from the steps to the skimmer and back, all in all, a whole lot of fun, more fun than I'd had in years.

After I'd been declared the winner, Barry went inside to check on what he said was a very important phone call, an act, I would realize later, absolved him of becoming a material witness. When the waves slowed to a steady calm, Doughboy and I sat on the steps in the shallow end, exhausted like fish washed up to shore. It was not something I'd thought about, not something I'd ever considered, but it seemed very natural for me to reach out and touch the narrow whiteness of his thigh. He was seventeen and not eighteen, and though he didn't seem to mind, my wife sure did, and that was the beginning of what became a long and unfair relationship with a storefront lawyer by the name of Boogie Bob Baldori. But my wife and I never divorced, and my daughter took my side in court, so the whole thing was not a loss. I've thought a lot about it since then, and those housing projects "serving the poor" are a big fat joke. And Doughboy did fine when he went back to community college, though I never heard from him again. I guess you could say I had something like a conversion experience, a baptism, if you will, a chance for a better life.

Acknowledgments

I would like to extend my sincere thanks to the editors of the magazines in which stories from this collection, sometimes in slightly different form, first appeared:

Evening Street Review: "The Dot";
Hayden's Ferry Review online: "Bun in the Oven";
J Journal: "Glue";
Limestone: "Adolescence in B Flat";
Quarterly West online: "Three Sad Stories";
Salt Hill: "Three Small Town Stories";
South Dakota Review: "The Love Feast";
StoryQuarterly: "Recipe for Disaster";
The Texas Observer online: "Three Stories of Prosperity";
Zone 3: "Remarkable."

Thanks also to Lisa Lewis, Joyce Freed Cox, Kenneth Cox, Amy Cox, Toni Graham, Nona Caspers, Dagoberto Gilb, Peter Conners, and the Department of English at Oklahoma State University.

About the Author

Dinah Cox's stories have appeared in such places as *StoryQuarterly, Prairie Schooner, Salt Hill, Cream City Review, Calyx, Copper Nickel, Beloit Fiction Journal,* and *Quarterly West,* and have won prizes from *The Atlantic Monthly, The Texas Observer,* and *Hayden's Ferry Review.* She teaches in the English Department at Oklahoma State University where she also is an associate editor at *Cimarron Review.* She lives and works in her hometown of Stillwater, Oklahoma.

BOA Editions, Ltd. American Reader Series

Colophon

BOA Editions, Ltd., a not-for-profit publisher of poetry and other literary works, fosters readership and appreciation of contemporary literature. By identifying, cultivating, and publishing both new and established poets and selecting authors of unique literary talent, BOA brings high-quality literature to the public. Support for this effort comes from the sale of its publications, grant funding, and private donations.

The publication of this book is made possible, in part, by the special support of the following individuals:

Anonymous x 3
Nin Andrews
Angela Bonazinga & Catherine Lewis
Nickole Brown & Jessica Jacobs
Bernadette Catalana
Christopher & DeAnna Cebula
Gwen & Gary Conners
Anne C. Coon & Craig J. Zicari
Gouvernet Arts Fund
Michael Hall, *in memory of Lorna Hall*
Grant Holcomb
Christopher Kennedy & Mi Ditmar
X. J. & Dorothy M. Kennedy
Keetje Kuipers & Sarah Fritsch, *in memory of JoAnn Wood Graham*
Jack & Gail Langerak
Daniel M. Meyers, *in honor of James Shepard Skiff*
Boo Poulin
Deborah Ronnen & Sherman Levey
Steven O. Russell & Phyllis Rifkin-Russell
Sue S. Stewart, *in memory of Stephen L. Raymond*
Lynda & George Waldrep
Michael Waters & Mihaela Moscaliuc
Michael & Patricia Wilder

Printed in the USA
CPSIA information can be obtained
at www.ICGtesting.com
JSHW082345140824
68134JS00020B/1898